these heavy lungs we breathe with

k.s. whittaker

cover art by Glen Nelson
title page art by Birdie Maxwell

kswhittaker.com

ISBN 978-0-9979594-9-9

for the one who put this deep ache inside me
that I could write about for centuries

preface

The impermanence of love was a thing I had to learn. It's not something you are taught from a young age. And as with any lesson, it comes with a resistance. This is about that resistance.

part one

Narrator: *You're a girl, not an animal.*

Valerie: *A she-mammal or a female child. I was on the border-line between human being and chaos.*

—Sarah Stridsberg

Chapter one

The lover destroyed

I have never known there to be so much talk surrounding the arrival of an Iraqi girl and her grandmother. But that's what came trailing in on their heels as they made a new home. The conversation, the rumors about their fortune, all of it clung to their backs even when they kept quiet in the evenings. I thought nothing of it. I was a miserable person. I saw ghosts around every corner. Ghosts of people I have lost, ghosts of people I know to be still alive, even ghosts of strangers. It was this town. I was ready to leave, run away and do whatever had to be done. I didn't have much to leave behind. Will my ghosts follow me? I was willing to take that risk. Willing to take the fall for a reckless decision on behalf of my anger, my resentment for all that has happened and will *happen*.

The orange trees in California seemed to never wither. The valley was bold and humid, harvesting anything but happiness, for the small town stifled any sort of dream you had. I was losing inspiration, writing down lists instead of poetry, investing time in failure rather than creativity. I had no muse. I was strangely okay with that. Okay with the idea of fruition finding me in another life. Maybe, in this life, I was not meant to create. Just *be*. I didn't need a symbol of my existence to be found like fossils. I put down the pen.

That day in math class, when my teacher handed me

back our last exam with a giant comical red D on the front page, I felt nothing. English class, my favorite, was next and oddly, I still felt nothing. I opened my journal, stared at the blank page and thought of *nothing*. I then closed the journal, frustrated. The new girl, sitting adjacent to me, flashed the A written on her exam to the boy sitting in front of me. He gave her a thumbs up. As the bell rang, I watched her get up and wander over to Michael's desk. I stuffed my exam into my bag, along with my journal, and made a run for it before my teacher could say anything.

The new girl began to appear everywhere. In every class, on the table beside me in the lunchroom, even at the cafe I spent most of my days. I couldn't shake this curiosity. I dropped my bag next to Samantha and sat down.

"Have you talked to the new girl?" I asked, letting the *curiosity* get the best of me.

"Yeah, she's nice." Samantha said.

"Does the new girl..."

"She has a name." Samantha laughed, turning to face me. Samantha was always the more social one, welcoming everyone and anyone into our friend group. I didn't even protest when she said she invited the new girl to Michael's party. I simply looked to where she stood across the schoolyard. The nonchalant way her hands spoke in the air when she was making a point. The way her long hazel hair glowed beneath the rays of the sun. Hearing her laugh like soft bells, I felt compelled to get to know her. To know her in a way that would ruin me completely. My curiosity was perhaps morbid.

I walked that day rather than riding my bike. I didn't wish to go home, knowing what was waiting for me. I made my way to the orange tree instead. Once there I stretched my arms out as I rested in the grass, retrieving a book from my bag. I read until the sun went down. When I eventually walked in through the front door, my dad was asleep. I sighed with relief and snuck quietly to my bedroom. I slept soundly. The nightmares were to come soon. But for now, I was happy to remain oblivious. I have known peace and it was mostly when I closed my eyes.

I didn't know how to feel about her. She picked up my pencil when I dropped it and she handed it back to me with a smile. A smile that seemed forced but harmless. It was always brief, our encounters. I was pretty certain she didn't even know I existed, with her quick witted remarks and unintentional shooing away. I could never forget her. Even if our time together did plan to flee.

I didn't know how to feel about her. She ran into me in the hallway and apologized without even looking in my direction. I didn't take it personally, but I was starting to grow impatient. Why did she not care to get to know me? Weary of my own approachability, I opened my locker and looked in the small mirror I had placed inside. I think I was friendly looking, well friendly enough. I grabbed my textbook for chemistry and shut my locker a little too forcefully.

I decided to despise her the night of Michael's party. It was cold and windy, the chimes that dangled made a clatter of noise while I shook with a joint in hand. Music blared from the house, the sound of glass breaking echoed and Michael ran inside. It was her hand that reached for mine as I passed the joint. She huffed with amusement when I nearly dropped it. I narrowed my eyes and looked at Samantha.

"I think he likes you." Ronny said.

"Who?" The new girl replied, still amused.

"Michael." Ronny murmured. I looked down at my feet. I thought Michael was an asshole. Ronny was jealous, I could tell by the way he said Michael's name.

All the boys liked *her*.

"Not my type." She remarked. I looked at her and our eyes met.

"What is your type? Boys or girls?" Samantha asked. Sexuality was Samantha's favorite topic, constantly wanting to tell everyone she experimented with a girl at summer camp years ago. I rolled my eyes and thought of going back inside where the crowd of people could hide my irritation.

The new girl blew out smoke and smiled.

"Boys. Just boys." She said smugly. I peered down at my feet and felt dizzy as the high began to kick in. It wasn't like me to feel so angry. I was not my father. I didn't even know why I felt such anger in the first place. I muttered something about getting a drink and stood up. Back inside I made my way to the bathroom and splashed cold water in my face. My

4

hair was curling from the wind outside so I ran my fingers through it, wincing at the pain of the knots. Maybe I was having a nervous breakdown from overstimulation. I closed my eyes and took a deep breath before opening the door. The new girl was standing there, twirling her long hair with one finger, leaning against the wall.

"All yours." I said, holding open the door.

"It's Ara, right?"

She did know me.

"Yeah. And you're Solene?"

"We have almost every class together." She said, ignoring my question. I said nothing. Smiling awkwardly, I started to walk in the direction of what I could only guess was a drunk Michael singing karaoke, hoping Solene would continue the conversation. I wanted her to give me a reason to stay in this hallway, away from the crowded room. But even if she did, the music would've silenced her as I kept walking. I never looked back.

My plan to hate her was crumbling with time. I settled with neutrality. I thought she was nice enough. I could even see us being friends. I decided to talk to her one day. I sat beside her in the schoolyard and listened to Samantha rant about their summer plans. Today was the last day of school.

"Hey, Ara." Solene eventually said.

"Hey." I said, "I was wondering if you two wanted to go swimming today?"

"Sounds fun." Solene said, smiling.

All three of us rode our bikes through town, past the field, past the orange tree, and out onto the sandy beach overlooking the lake. The sky was golden. Solene hops off her bike, waving us over as she runs to the water, removing her top. And this, *this* is probably where I could've prevented it. Could've spared so much of myself when it came to the girl right in front of me. But at that moment, I thought nothing of it. Samantha follows suit, shouting, "Come on, Ara." They both scream and laugh at the cold touch of the water. I willingly jumped in.

Afterwards, we lay on the dock. It was sunset. My hair was nearly dry. Samantha and Solene are talking about boys. Solene had apparently been seeing Michael and they shared their first kiss last night. I closed my eyes and listened to the water gently hit into the wood.

"I should be getting home." I said.

"Me too. My grandma will be worried." Solene muttered, standing up.

"How's your father..." Samantha whispered as we got dressed.

"Not now, Sam." I said. I didn't want anyone to know of my troubles. Solene's house happened to be in the same direction as mine. Samantha said her goodbye and I got onto my bike, knees wobbly. Solene gripped my shoulder as I started to fall. She squeezed gently, just gentle enough to make me think I made the whole thing up. I shivered and looked at her. She smiled. Her teeth were white, her front tooth a little crooked in a way I found charming.

"Be careful." She said, "Ready?"

"Yeah." I was embarrassed by my clumsiness. She took off ahead and I watched her throw her head back with her mouth wide, still smiling for a reason I did not know. That was the summer we inevitably became inseparable. That was the summer I completely lost myself.

In a journal of hers, Plath said *I may never be happy, but tonight I am content*. I felt *that* when I was with Solene. I felt content enough to stow sorrow in my back pocket and forget it by nightfall. When it did come to rear its head, it looked like my mother. How could I despise my own sadness when it resembled the only scrap of her I had left? But on a day where I was content, I knew the reason was this; a ripe orange in Solene's hands as she read fiction to me. I just liked how she said things. The way she pronounced certain vowels, the way she stretched out a word that had great meaning, and of course the shyness in it all because we were new to this. New to being friends. I read to her in return, laughing whenever she made unnecessary commentary. We ate the bread she brought from home, her grandmother's secret recipe. We shared clothes, I told her to not even bother to pack anything but a toothbrush whenever she slept over. I snuck her into my house each night so my father wouldn't be a problem. We spent every second of every day together, listening to sad music and riding bikes to all corners of our small town. She was slowly becoming someone vital in my life. Vital in a way that frightened me, because I didn't know what my life looked like before her. I could only remember being a lifeless meteor that hemorrhaged through a downhearted atmosphere. I now had a best friend who understood me and took care of me. I took care of her, too. And it was all happening rapidly. Our friendship was a rapid thing that I never, even once, saw coming.

"I think you should go on a double date with me and Michael."

"Who would I go with?"

"Ronny."

I laughed, hysterically. Solene joined in, nudging my shoulder.

"C'mon, I'm being serious."

"I'm being serious too." I said, wiping away my smile.

"What's so bad about Ronny?"

"Solene..." I groaned. I've known Ronny since I was nine. He was the kid who stuck pencils in his ears. Not even a single ounce of me found him attractive.

"Okay, fine." Solene said.

"I like how things are right now. The last thing I need is a relationship." I said, lightheartedly.

"Fair enough."

I wanted to warn her about Michael and the things I knew about him. But I didn't want to overstep. I continued reading my book while I felt her staring. I didn't question the chills it gave me. I didn't question the pulling sensation I felt on the sides of my mouth, as if her *stare* made me involuntarily smile.

"What?" She asked, a slight giggle bubbling under the surface of her concern.

"Nothing." I shrugged.

"Bullshit." She said, opening up her own book.

"You were staring..."

"Was I?"

"Yeah."

"Sorry."

"I don't mind."

"Okay." She smiled.

"Okay?"

"I was staring because you look happy." She paused, "Happier than when I first met you."

I don't know why but I winced. Maybe I winced because I didn't know that my own miserable self rubbed off on others, or was detected.

"I'm only *slightly* happy." I said. Our eyes met and then we were laughing again.

"You make me happy." Solene said after our laughter died down.

"I'm happy to know you." I said in return. The silence that came after made me think I fucked it up. My honesty, at times, felt like a fatal flaw. Though, at times, everything that came out of my mouth felt like a lie. I didn't want to scare her off with an overbearing heart. I forgot what it was like to care for someone so vivaciously. We had become sisters. But the word *sisters* stuck with me noisily, as if to say *wrong*,

wrong, wrong. Friends felt fitting. *Friends.* Still, the noise was there.

I loved everything and everyone, quite suddenly. I was writing more than ever, observing others and keeping my head down to listen to conversation. It inspired me, *life*. Life was now a thing that proved to be worth living. I loved everything and everyone, inexplicably. Happiness was running rampant in my body. Though happiness felt foreign, I let it smother me. And I hoped Solene felt it, too. Sharing most of our days, my happiness had to have been contagious. But there was always something, in the back of my mind, that gorged on weariness. I still had the same life. The same circumstances. Solene was bound to make a run for it if she found out too much. I kept my secrets close to my chest. I kept this happiness a secret until the very end. Until it was taken away. There was some kind of rotten thing hiding within me.

The anniversary of my mother's death was on this day. That's when the whiskey occupied my father and I would lock myself in my room. He was a drunk, a mean drunk, but today he was a weeping drunk. I felt bad, unable to face him or comfort him because I looked too much like her. What a waste. We could've grown closer. Instead, I was nearly seventeen, soft spoken and afraid for my life. No one knew about my father's habits besides Samantha. She was the one who had to hear him almost break down my door when I locked it. She was the one who hugged me after my father called me an ungrateful bitch and threw the tv remote at the wall. So of all days, it was today that hurt most when Solene showed up at my front door in a yellow dress. I stepped out and shut the door quietly, not to disturb my father who was now sleeping.

"You haven't been answering my texts." Solene frowned.

"I'm sorry."

"I missed you." She sounded breathless.

"Let's meet at our spot tomorrow?" *Our spot*, a simple orange tree among a flourishing field. I only showed it to the ones I trusted most.

"Not today?"

"Today doesn't work for me." I felt pain for rejecting her. She was biting her bottom lip. She looked concerned.

"Okay." She said after a slight pause. I was relieved she didn't question me further. So when I showed up to the orange tree the next day I had no reason to collapse in her arms crying. But I did anyway. She soothed me like a best friend, rocking me like I suppose a mother would. Was I crying because it had all come crashing down? My mother, my father, my secret life that I led. I was only a child most days, with no sense of direction. Solene never asked what was wrong and I was grateful for that. I didn't want her pity nor her understanding.

Solene and I didn't speak of my episode. Since that night, I was becoming someone I was unfamiliar with. The hunger pains came and went, I was starved for something I could not name. I know now that the nightmares began not too long after she materialized. The kind of nightmares that make sleep dreadful. The kind that tore at your psyche like ravaged wolves. My mind was so full of grief, an exorcism was taking place within my dreams to get it out. I came to the conclusion that *this* was a punishment. *A punishment for what?* I had no idea. Not yet, at least.

Solene was reading Plath beside me, brow furrowed. She did that when she read. I didn't realize I was staring until she said, "Why are you staring?" "Nothing. Just getting hungry." I wasn't hungry.

"Eat an orange." She stood up and plucked a single orange from a low hanging branch, and tossed it to me. I ate it quickly once it was peeled. The sweetness of the orange was intoxicating.

"What are you reading?" Solene asked.

"Zami."

Solene took the book from where it sat beside me. I looked at her, confused. She put *my* book into her bag and smiled. I didn't even ask why she was stealing it. I was slightly amused. We were sitting close to one another, the blanket we brought was far too small. I noticed *her eyes*, brown with specks of green and honey. I also couldn't help but notice her lips were stained a cherry red, her hazel hair wavy. That unfamiliarity crept back in and I shook my head.

"It's getting late." I said.

"Here, you're supposed to take my book now." She said, handing it to me.

"Why?"

"I'll annotate yours and you'll annotate mine. Then we'll give them back to each other." She smiled. I reluctantly took her copy of *Ariel*, though I've read it dozens of times. I was willing to play her game. Solene then stood up, brushing dirt and grass off her shorts. She grabbed my now sticky hand and helped me up. It was nearly dark outside and my father's disdain could be felt for miles. It was past my curfew. How do I tell her that I live a lie, with my father's teeth clamped down around me? There was no place safe but here. *Solene, I'm afraid.* Our hands were still twined. I pulled away with a little too much aggression.

"Goodnight, Ara." Solene said, climbing onto her bike. Later that night, I opened Solene's book and began to read, highlighting and writing all my thoughts to the point where the pages were completely full. *I am terrified by this dark thing that sleeps in me.* In response to Plath I wrote, *the thing that sleeps in me is rage.* I hoped Solene would understand. Did she know what it was like to be rage-filled? To be brimming with an anger that suffocates the softness I so desperately try to evoke. I finished the book by four a.m. and fell asleep holding it in my arms. My dreams that night were painless but nonetheless still frightening. I was guilty for dreaming of death. *Solene, what if I tell you that I feel like dying, but I'll do nothing about it?*

To this day, I know Solene was not a ghost. Just the embodiment of all my ghosts trapped in human form. Though I felt crazy, I knew she would understand. I never spoke of it, my ghosts, my skeletons in the closet. I never once brought up my mother and father. I never once imagined *my punishment* to be inflicted by her. *Never once* imagined my feelings to be deeper than *this*. I ignored it until I could no longer do so. Whatever *this* was. Unfamiliar territory. I plotted hard to forget *this*. Later on I would put a name to it. *Yearning.* Castigation followed.

"I dream of running away." Solene said.

"Where would you go?" I asked. My stomach dropped at the thought of her leaving.

"No idea. You can come. And of course my grandmother would come, too."

I snorted.

"That's not running away, Solene."

"At least it will take me far away from here."

"What's not to like?"

"The town is so small and stuffy. I can't breathe." She sighed. That was the first time she ever brought up wanting to run away. It made me wonder even more of her past. *Are you so inconsolable, Solene, that you won't even let me take care of you?* I was gripped by sympathy, my throat tightening as I wished to mend her. *I'm not broken*, I can hear her say.

I did not know how to explain it. I was envious of the way she got under my skin. I ached at the sight of her. I was deprived of such friendship since Samantha and I had grown apart. It was my fault. I was too wrapped up in fading away, hiding myself in books and my journal. But I couldn't hide from Solene, I couldn't bear to not be seen by her. Still unfamiliar, I told myself I was aching to be reminded of a time where I was seen as human. All the boys who saw me as meat. All the girls who saw me as threatening. I remember Amber said I was a cunt because her boyfriend wanted my number. I was human, I was. Solene made me feel human. I ached because I was ready to walk into a room and look for her in every corner. I was wanting to ache, openly and readily.

My copy of Zami was returned to me a week later. A single page was dog eared. I turned to the page eagerly and read the part she had underlined. *I was discovering all the ways that love creeps into life when two selves exist closely, when two women meet.* I blushed. I couldn't remember the last time I had ever blushed. I flipped through the rest of the book and read all her notes she left in the margins. I didn't know why I felt so warm. I was ignited by this unfamiliar feeling of kinship. This feeling of lust. *Lust?* Of course, I was blind from the beginning. *Solene.* I was *now* familiar with a self that maybe, just *maybe*, wanted her. I was at least ready to admit that my feelings surpassed whatever we were now. *Best friends? Solene.* I was scared out of my mind. I *was* smitten. I now remember smitten to be akin to the word *smite*. To be beaten, bruised, stricken. So then does smitten mean to be devastatingly struck by adoration? The devastation to come was proof enough.

I rode my bike past the field on a day where I felt like hiding in plain sight. I looked to the right. Solene was under *the* orange tree. I wanted to join her and tell her *I feel on fire. I only feel it when I'm around you. Why is that?* Despite my need to ask these questions, I turned around and headed home. She'll never know how the bright oranges paled in comparison to her slender body as she lounged in the grass, drowning out the world with a book in hand, swimming in a sea of languished secrets. Her suffering was quite prominent, but her confidence was brave. I glanced back one last time and she was gone. *My Eurydice.* All that had gone unnoticed before was now obvious. Her beauty? *Obvious.* Her voice? How could her voice sound like the moon? I did not think I knew the moon's language, but now I am hungry for it.

I just wanted her *bliss.* To continue in this perfect bubble we created. Our friendship, though brittle at times, was perfect. With these new feelings that had come alive, there was nothing I could do about it. My dreams had escalated. Solene now became a part of them. We were wandering through an ancient city. Reading on the seven hills. Feeding from Lupa. Skinny dipping in the Tyrrhenian Sea. We prayed in the Pantheon. I told strangers about our forbidden love. And once we did all that we could do to save one another, I was betrayed as was Rome when Tarpeia spoke to the Sabines. *I will be betrayed.* I didn't want to believe it. Who was Solene? Just someone I now desire? We rarely spoke of personal things. She was infuriating at times, pure at others. I couldn't decide what I was feeling most days. We were no more than strangers. Solene knew nothing about me and I knew nothing about her. Why did she care so much, showing up at my doorstep every single day? Why did she stick around when I was such a miserable person? Perhaps my thoughts were apparent because Solene nudged me in that moment and smiled. That same smile I couldn't help but mirror. We were under the orange tree. The heat was blistering.

"What's up?" She asked.

"Nothing." I muttered, already defensive.

"If you say so."

"Why haven't I met your grandmother?"

Solene looked at me, confused.

"You always talk about her..."

"She doesn't know English." Solene said. "What would you two talk about?"

"Nevermind." I snapped.

"Hey, what's your problem Ara?"

"Nothing. Just... I'm sorry. I didn't get much sleep last night."

"Okay."

"Okay?"

"Try to be a little more nice to me sometimes." Solene said, pouting.

"I'm sorry, Solene."

"My grandmother is a serious woman. She's eighty five and is set in her ways. But she'd like you." Solene smiled. "I know she would."

I felt the anger wash away all at once and I almost reached for her hand.

"I miss my country." Solene said, solemnly, after a great

deal of silence between us. "Even though it took everything from me, I still miss it."

"I miss my mom." I whispered. Solene is now the one who takes my hand and squeezes it. She's the first person I've said that to in years. I wanted to know all her demons. I wanted to kiss the sadness from her mouth and carry it myself. I wanted to taste the nape of her neck and ask her everything there is to ever know about a person. A girl like Solene deserved an ocean, not a raging river that was shallow. Her heart was deep. It could hold the entire Atlantic. I squeezed her hand. *Solene, have your way with me.* She said nothing for the rest of the day.

She always asked to walk me home from the orange tree or the cafe or anywhere we went together. I was territorial. I hoped she knew these were our *spaces*. Only for us. It was nearing the end of summer and I was infatuated. The kind of infatuation that makes you smile too much and makes other people sick. The only problem was, nobody knew and nobody could ever know. It was my secret to keep. Yet sometimes the yearning grew so large, I felt outnumbered. *The way she would quote poetry to me. The way I would lean in, catching myself in a thought so unseemly that I could feel my cheeks burn red. The way she would stare back at me and I'd think: Do you feel it too? Do you feel this hunger that is eating me alive?* Tell me I'm not crazy, Solene. I write furiously in my journal, not about us, no, there can't be any trace of *us*. But I do write about the birds that sing too loud in the morning and the bees that made a home in the yard. How strange it is to notice and appreciate the small things when life is so clear. *You make me good, Solene. For you, I will be good.*

On a day where I chose to hide again, Michael came to the orange tree looking for Solene. That was the moment I realized she had brought him here before. I felt ill. I told him I didn't know where she was, then I packed my bag and left. This place felt hollow now. Solene called me later that night and I ignored all four calls. I wanted to throw my phone, just as my father threw the remote, I wanted to break everything. I wanted to puke and cry and get her back for all the pain she has caused. But I was weak, thoughtless. How could I ever be good enough for her? As the phone rang a fifth time, I blinked away my tears and picked it up.

I answered with a disgruntled hello. Solene was sobbing hysterically. She had never cried in all the time I have known her. My pulse was racing. After minutes of calming her down, I could finally understand her.

"What took you so long to answer?" She wailed.

"I was busy." My heart sank down into my stomach.

"Are you upset with me?" She asked, voice shaky.

"Solene..."

"Can you meet me?"

I wanted to suggest that she call Michael but my cynical side was not pretty. I agreed to see her.

Solene was sitting on her ratty blanket that we always laid on. Her face was puffy from crying but there were no longer tears leaking from her eyes. I was dreading this part, this part of not knowing who or what had hurt her. *If it was me, Solene, please forgive me for every fiber of my being needs you to be okay.* I sit beside her and feel the tension immediately. She's breathing softly, evenly, and I feel as though my breath is ragged. I could die right here and she still would never know how I feel.

"Ara..." She began. How my name falls off her lips, I could melt from the ease of it all. "...Have I ever told you of my country?"

"No."

"I promise someday I will tell you everything. It's hard to talk about. Everything that has happened to me. I feel so helpless. But Ara, you have to say you'll always be my friend. You can't abandon me."

I could say, *there's no leaving even if I wanted to. Even if I wanted to rid of you, there's no going back to the way my life was before. There's no cure to get you out of my anatomy. You're built into me, Solene.*

Instead, I say, "You're my closest friend."

She hugs me tight and we stay like this, tangled, until both our curfews. But at this very moment, I hoped that would never come. I hoped the sun would never set. I hoped she knew. Knew just how much I almost *said it* every time I saw her. On a whim, I almost said *I love you. The escalation of this feeling was swift and transformative. I love you. The escalation of you was boundless in a way I could never have foreseen.* I never would have plummeted into her if I knew what was to come.

Chapter two

The ledge

Dreaming of the world coming to an end would have been alarming, if it weren't for the fact it felt like my world had ended on numerous occasions. Motherless, unrequited love, and now Solene is standing right in front of me saying her period is late. Late as in she's been sleeping with Michael all summer and the condom broke. I did my best to disguise my disgust with genuine worry, afraid for my friend and her now doomed future. I even go above and beyond by being the one to buy the pregnancy test. It's a small town, everyone will talk. My father will be too drunk to listen.

"It says to pee on it for ten seconds." I whisper. We were standing in Solene's bathroom, her grandmother is in the kitchen making Knafeh for us. I had wanted to meet her grandmother for so long, but not like this. She was a painter, her hands thin and frail. Solene proudly hung all her paintings in her bedroom, pointing to the date tree that was outside their family home in Iraq.

"Sex before marriage is a sin to my grandmother. She'll kill me if she finds out..."

"Then why did you do it?" I said without thinking. Solene glanced down at the pregnancy test that was now on the counter and then looked back at me with disappointment.

"I don't need your judgment."

"You don't even follow the religion."

"I try to *follow* what my grandmother says. I care what she says."

"I'm sorry."

"Ara, I'm scared."

"Don't freak out now."

Minutes passed by with complete silence, I couldn't bring myself to look anywhere but my shoes. *Solene, if this is true, if this test is positive, I'm not sure how much more I can take.*

"Negative!" Solene said, grabbing my waist and pulling me into her. Her breasts were heaving with relief and I felt so much peace. Closing my eyes, I breathed in her scent. Always cinnamon.

"Let's have you meet Vinos." She said, turning to the door. I wanted to fall to my knees. I would've begged right then and there if I knew it would get me what I wanted.

Once in the kitchen, Solene and her grandmother exchanged some words as I stood off in the corner. The room was warm and familiar. Vinos looked over at me and smiled, a kindness that a stranger has never offered. She was tall, just like Solene, wisps of silver hair protruding from her Hijab. I held up my hand, a weak excuse for an introduction. Solene went to my side and nodded, nudging my shoulder. Vinos' smile grew. Solene spoke some more in Arabic, her first language, so beautiful and raw. I tightened my fist in reaction to the violent wave of *want* that sifted through me. I'd like to believe that we were as gritty as the salt that covers the sea.

We spent the rest of the night eating, talking, and laughing; Solene translated so Vinos and I could get to know each other. Offering up the seat next to mine, Solene moved to the other side of the table while her grandmother stood to approach me. I didn't know what was happening. She then took my hands into hers.

"انتي خليتي سولين كلش سعيد." Vinos said, nodding contentedly. I looked to Solene, who was now blushing. I chose to never ask what it meant.

"Are you still seeing Michael?" I said. We were in her room on opposite ends of the bed. She was reading my copy of *The Waves* when suddenly she flipped onto her back.

"There was a star riding through clouds one night, and I said to the star, 'Consume me'." Solene looked over at me. I need to rebuild my bravery, I am remade, painfully, each night when the confession falters. *I'll give you the stars if that's what you truly want. I'll consume you.*

"And no, I haven't seen Michael in awhile." Solene says, burying her face back into the book. I try not to gloat. I returned to my journal and wrote down her name for the first time. I find her staring again.

"What?"

"Does that make you happy?"

I was caught.

"Writing in that journal? Does it make you happy?" She said. I was now afraid she would push me further and ask to read what was inside.

23

"Yes, it makes me happy." But I wanted to say, what makes me *truly* happy is that orange tree and *you*, *you*, *you*. This question roused feelings in me that must've remained dormant for so long. A cup of coffee, a poem, canyons with lush vegetation, bike rides in the heat; the little things in my life that remind me of *you*. I'm spellbound by the ease of our life together.

Sometimes I think I'm not human. Just rage bundled up into flesh, touch starved and wretched. I am wretched for the way my father can't love me, for the way Solene can't know me, for the way my mother left me. And on days like this, where I lock myself away in my room to write or read, I think the pain is unbearable. I hear my father walk down the hall, maybe with his ear pressed against my door, he can hear my heart race. I hear a timid knock and I say, "Come in."

"Where's your friend?" He asked, standing awkwardly in the doorway.

"I don't know."

"Any plans tonight?"

"No."

This was how the majority of our conversations went. His small talk was a slap in the face. Did he forget how last night he slurred my mother's name while I was busy cleaning up all his bottles?

"We can watch a movie tonight?" He suggested. I would have laughed if his kindness wasn't so demeaning. I loved my father, I truly did, but his verbal abuse and lack of care throughout the years had a numbing effect on me.

"Sure." I still craved his approval, his attention.

We sat beside each other on the couch. I chose a lighthearted movie, holding my breath because he was hiding alcohol in a mug, sipping at a dangerous speed. He only made it halfway through before he passed out. I took the mug to wash it. Whiskey again. I felt my stomach turn. Crawling into my bed, I pressed my face into the pillow as if I was ready to scream. I never have the courage, it's getting so old.

The last week of summer came and I held on tight. Solene was waiting for me as I dashed outside. The afternoon was swelling with humidity and lust, I kicked up my bike stand and followed her down the road. I was aware of the fragility of our time together, for youth was ever so waning. I imagined Solene with a husband, a picket fence, four kids and a husky. I almost smiled at the simplicity of it. Though cumbersome, I still wanted what was best for her. But there is nothing settled. Our prospects, our humanity; all is defiant.

"What's wrong?" Solene's question, her voice, felt like a hand running through my hair.

"It's my father..."

"He's an alcoholic." She simply stated.

"Sam told you, didn't she?" I said. Solene gave me a look.

"Why didn't you say anything? All this time, and..."

"It's no one's business." We leave it at that but I can feel her *hurt* enter my bloodstream, and I'm infected for the rest of the night. I lie awake in bed. I toss, I turn, I fret, and I feel haunted by her absence. How lonely it is to be a woman.

My father was tearing off the wallpaper in the spare bedroom when I woke up for school. Maybe it was for the best, this house was a shrine to all that we had lost. I ignored his look of concern as I dragged my feet into the bathroom, sleep deprived and foggy. The dreams were becoming vivid and grotesque; an angel pushed down a stairwell and the blood drained from their ears. The orange tree rotting. The earth splitting into two. Solene *touching* me. I wake up entirely aroused. School was the last thing I needed. The year would go on predictably. Solene would go to a different college, far away. A new boy will take over and I'll be left to clean up the mess. I was suddenly sick, gripping the bathroom sink, breathing through my nose when my phone buzzed. *Coffee before class?* It was Solene. I fled my house before I gave my father a reason to yell.

"How did your mother die, Ara?"

"If I tell you, will you tell me one thing about you?" I said.

"Sure."

"I've never told anyone this before..."

"Not even Sam?"

"Not even Sam." I looked down at the road and pushed my bike along the gravel. "My mother was depressed for quite some time. So when she killed herself, it wasn't a surprise."

"Wasn't your mother Christian?"

"Yeah."

"And she..."

"Yeah." I nodded.

"How did she do it?" She paused, "Fuck, I'm sorry, I didn't mean to ask that..."

"An overdose."

"I'm sorry, Ara."

"That's why I don't tell anyone. Because of how you're looking at me right now."

"I'll make it even. I'll tell you how I lost my family."

"Only if you want to."

"I want to."

We both stopped in place, facing each other.

"The military hung them in a tree and then set their bodies on fire. I came home from school and found them dead." We walked the rest of the way in silence.

One Sunday when Vinos was out shopping, Solene and I spent a lazy afternoon in her room. Listening to music, highlighting favorite quotes from books scattered about. It was my futile attempt at getting these words through to her head. And amidst the futility of it all, I still looked up to her as if she were the sun. She *was* the sun. But to burn too bright for too long, she might just fade away. *I'll offer up all my light, Solene. I'll ask for nothing in return.*

Caught in my own trance, I hardly noticed when she came and laid next to me. Her window was wide open, the

27

early autumn air trickling in. I shivered.

"Are you cold?" Before I could answer, she was taking off her oversized hoodie.

"Thank you." I said, putting it on in one motion, devoured by the scent of cinnamon. *Her* scent. It wasn't until later that night that I reveled in it. Alone in my room, I pulled it halfway over my head, blinded by the fabric, completely inebriated by the smell, letting my hands rest beneath my underwear. I began to touch myself, careless in the way I said her name, breathing in the cinnamon; my hands became *her* hands. I then bit down into the fabric as I climaxed, pulsating my hips to the sensation of my fingers working their way in and out. Minutes go by before I can no longer stand the amount of pleasure. My veins were on fire. I remove my hand, I remove the hoodie, tossing it far off into the corner, and I allow my breathing to catch up to itself. I am now repulsed. And in that repulsion, I shower in scalding water, scrubbing my skin until it nearly bleeds.

I was growing weary of my fixation, nervous to see it swallow me whole. The next day I felt determined to move on. I put the hoodie into the washer and washed away her scent. I knew it was for the best. At school I steered clear of her. It was only temporary. Just until this crush of mine willingly left. *I will not abandon you. But Solene, all the darkest parts of myself are brought forth like vines to strangle me.* Did she see right through me? Did she see past the facade as I stowed away behind my books and counterfeit lifestyle? I felt like a corpse. I used to want to pursue creative writing when I got to college. I used to listen to my favorite songs and felt inspired to live. I used to *live*. But somehow, along the way, my flame was extinguished. Growing up was a mistake.

"Where's Solene?" Samantha asked. In my new state of loneliness, I invited Samantha to the orange tree. The hollow feeling in my chest had not subsided since Solene and I's last encounter.

"Haven't heard from her." It wasn't true. She had texted and called. I ignored every single one of them, white knuckled.

"Strange." Samantha said.

Heedless, I looked to the orange tree and said, "When you slept with that girl at summer camp, was she the only one?"

"No." Samantha giggled. "Why do you ask?"

"Is there a difference..." I swallowed. "Between sleeping with a man or woman?"

"What kind of question is that?"

"Sam, just humor me for a moment." I had not stopped staring at the orange tree.

"Well, for me it was different, yeah."

"How?"

"Girls have a certain softness about them." She became more animated. "They know all the right spots." I listened to her go in depth about the art of intimacy that these girls seemed to have mastered. I thought of how all the sleepovers I've had, from a young age, were never easy. Being friends with girls was never *easy*. And the truth of that, that I was facing right now, scared me. I then thought of Solene and felt my thighs ache. That scared me even more. Was it possible to carry on like this? Only catching glimpses of *her* in hallways. Only left with the ghost of *us*. Only left with the ghosts that Solene helped me forget.

Later that night I pulled out my phone and read through Solene's string of texts.

Hi, where are you?

Ara?

Are you ignoring me?

Miss you!

Just let me know if everything's alright.

I typed out, *Everything is falling apart without you. You're my muse and my universe, without you I have nothing left. Solene, you'll never know how much I love you. I love you, I love you, please do whatever you want with me.* I shook my head and forcefully erased it. I instead type out, *I'm okay.* She replied almost immediately. *Do you want to talk about it?*

Not really, I say. I then silenced my phone as I nestled into my bed. The yearning would not cease. I, at last, give in. I am now overcome with an appetite so fierce, I grip my sheets and shut my eyes. Love should not gnaw so heavenly.

"I forgive you for treating me like shit." Solene said. It was a rainy Tuesday, the smell of wet grass permeated the air. I didn't know how to respond. As if she knew I was trapped inside my head, Solene pushed me playfully and I grimaced. She found that to be humorous.

"You're hurting me." I said. Her face contorted into worry.

"Ara, I was just…"

"I know." I sighed. I felt foolish for my reaction.

"Are you okay?"

No, I wasn't in the slightest. I had this internal black hole I could not escape.

"Sometimes I think I'm so miserable, Solene, that I just might ruin everything good in my life." I said it in a rush, pulling my knees to my chest.

"You won't ruin me." She smiled. I could have kissed her a thousand times in this moment and it still would not have been enough.

Life was happening without me and all the things I used to numb myself were slowly becoming ineffective. I grieved in all the wrong ways. Grieved for my mother by attempting to forget her. Grieved for my innocence by not telling a soul of all those who have touched me wrong. Grieved my sexuality, my body, my way of eating. It all came full circle and caught me red handed. For the most part, I had always been okay with the lack of sensation. But that had all changed once Solene happened to me, no longer wanting to drown out the silence. I was now willing to *try*. What did it mean to lead a life that had so many planned tomorrows? Not quite healed, I was still finding that part out. Slowly but surely, I was becoming *whole* for her.

We were basking on the dock. The sun borrowed from July was vibrant, and I could feel her body next to mine. Solene was quiet today but I knew better than to ask when she was like this. I knew her moods like the back of my hand. That's why it surprised me when she rolled on her side to face me.

"Are you a virgin?" Solene asked.

"You're joking, right?" I laughed, nervously.

"I'm serious." She lightheartedly sulked.

"That's why you've been moping around all day? Because you wanted to know about my sex life?"

"I haven't been moping!"

"Solene..." I wanted her to drop it.

"You're so secretive when it comes to these things. Just talk to me."

I thought of what I could tell her, how I wanted to die every time a boy touched me, how every boy who had touched me took advantage. "There's been a few." I said. "Your turn."

"Just Michael, actually."

"Michael was your first?"

"Hey, don't judge!"

"Did you like it...with him?"

"Yeah, I suppose." She smiled, as if the flashbacks even brought her pleasure. The thought of somebody else touching her was unfathomable.

"Solene, just be careful."

"Okay mom." Solene rolled her eyes. Was I nothing more to her than that? Just a motherly friend who cares about when and who she sleeps with? I wished I could be more. So much more. *I could feel it radiate through my limbs.* What *more* did I have to do to show her? What more did I have to sacrifice? I looked down at my hands. These hands that should have known what it was like to hold her. I felt helpless. Uneasy, I rolled off the dock and into the water. I didn't come up for air. I didn't panic. I just let myself be submerged. When survival kicked in, I swam to the surface and started gasping. Solene was now standing on the dock, furious.

"What?"

"I thought you were hurt!" Solene said, "I was ready to jump in."

"I was just swimming." I laughed, climbing back up the ladder.

"Okay."

She'll never know how much I wanted to sink to the bottom. It wasn't about drowning. It was about the way the water helped me forget my thoughts. As if they just could float. Truth was, we both had tendencies that lean towards death. *Solene, I won't keep score if you don't.*

Throughout fall I missed the intense pining that came along with summer. The kind of pining the poets spoke of, as if anything could compare so feverishly to her hands that fell close to the equator. When winter comes, then what?

Bereft of the mutual heat between two lovers, shall I freeze?
What will the ice do to my lungs that breathe her very air?
These questions tugged so deeply at my heartstrings; a silent
reminder that I was *alive*.

"When you return I am going to give you one literary
fuck fest." Solene said. "God, Henry Miller was romantic."

I snorted. "You find anyone with a pen to be romantic."
Solene set down her book and looked at me.

"I have an idea."

"A fuck fest?"

"Let's get drunk. I know where my grandmother hides
her wine."

Before I could answer, she was out the room and down
the hallway.

"Won't she be home soon?" I called out.

"She'll be back from errands later. What she doesn't
know won't hurt."

Vinos never questioned what we did in Solene's room.
She only came in to offer food, smiling warmly with the
kind of motherly affection I missed most.

"Let loose." Solene said, walking back into the room,
swigging from a bottle of red wine. I took it from her and
put my lips to it. *The closest we'll ever get.*

"Okay but if I'm hungover tomorrow..."

"I'm a dead man, got it."

Our eyes met as I passed back the bottle. Aside from
that night at Michael's, this will be a first. Intoxicated and
alone. I felt high strung in the sense that anything could

happen. And by the second bottle, I was already daring.

"Sam told me *girls have a certain softness*."

"Is that so?" Solene arched her brow.

"I wouldn't know." I shrugged, detracting.

"In my country, that's not something we can talk about." Solene frowned. I nodded. I understood. The room was spinning. And in a morbid way, I looked at her red stained mouth and imagined it decorating me with adoration. *I just need you, in a quiet way that feasts on desperation.*

"What was that letter you were reading earlier, the one by Henry Miller?"

"The one he wrote to Anais?"

"Read it to me." I was growing braver by the second.

"Okay." Solene smirked, reaching for the book that was splayed out on the ground. "When you return I am going to give you one literary fuck fest— that means fucking and talking and talking and fucking— and a bottle of Anjou in between— or a Vermouth Cassis. Anaïs, I am going to open your very groins. God forgive me if this letter is ever opened by mistake. I can't help it. I want you. I love you. You're food and drink to me— the whole bloody machinery, as it were. Lying on top of you is one thing, but getting close to you is another. I feel close to you, one with you, you're mine whether it is acknowledged or not."

"You're right. Romantic." I said, sincerely.

"We're swooning over Henry Miller's erection."

We laughed instantaneously, limbs colliding and before I knew it she was lying on top of me.

"You're drunk." I said, aware of how close our mouths suddenly were.

"So are you." She said, pushing the hair from my face.

I nearly gave in, her hot breath against my skin, I was struck with instant melancholy. And just as fast as it happened, it ended. There was a knock on Solene's door. She bolted forward and shouted something in arabic. The room was still spinning.

I was aware of my obsession, whether it be in a crowded room or on a lonely street. I was always looking for her, painfully aware. And I saw this obsession to be innocent, as innocent as any fantasy goes. Although lonely, I actually have never felt so full. Each morning I had my coffee and toast, staring at the wall. My mind consumed with the constant dream of Solene and I making love in a burning field while the world ended. *My sweet doomsday, I'll hold you in the flood; through all the earthquakes and famine, I won't let this act of God tear us apart.* I did not want to make a bad habit out of daydreaming, but I couldn't help it; our contact was rusting since our drunken night together. Our bodies barely brushed, dwindling like a terminally ill patient; I was malnourished. A punishment for the rage I was encased in. I felt monstrous and tense. Chaos came alive within me from the moment I entered girlhood. How could I ever be loved? *Solene, don't pit my desire and fury against me.*

We were taking advantage of what was left of the warm fall weather by spending most days at the orange tree.

Lazing in the dead grass as we recited our favorite passages to one another, drinking sweet tea and listening to Mistki. But today, the air felt different.

"I started seeing Michael again." Solene said, casually.

"I know you brought him here." I said. I couldn't help it.

"What does it matter?" Solene laughed. "It's just a tree."

I did not answer, afraid my voice might break. Instead, I stand up to leave. Solene grabbed my wrist and pulled me.

"Let me go." I snapped, defeated by the way her touch overcame me with rapture. Even in the face of anger, I could never hate Solene.

"Ara, c'mon."

"If this tree is nothing, then what am I?" I was blubbering before I knew it, pushing her away as I went to hide my face. I didn't know why I was crying, I just felt all emotion collapse within me and I could not suppress it any longer. "God, I'm sorry. Just ignore me." I stuttered, feeling like my lungs might just burst.

"How could I ever ignore you." Solene said.

"You can be quite good at it." I sounded bitter. Solene rolled her eyes and put down the book she held in one hand.

"What's that supposed to mean, Ara?"

"Nothing."

"Just say it."

"No."

"You have to. You've interrupted my reading, you're

crying, and now I'm pissed. Just say it."

I threw my hands up and sighed. How could this all be coming to an end so quickly? How do I say what I feel in so few words? *Forgive me, Solene.*

"You're like this disease..."

"A disease?"

"Yes! A disease that has plagued me and I don't know how to recover!"

Solene nodded, wide eyed at my outburst. *Let's go back to summer, Solene. Let's go back to when you were kissing Michael and I was just the enamored girl who kept her mouth shut.*

"Romantic." Solene finally said. I groaned and looked toward the sunset. The sky was pink.

I expected a harsh exchange of words, for her to retreat. But nothing. And then suddenly she was kissing my cheek. No mystery at all, just a friendly peck. I remained wordless.

"I'm not sure how to recover either." She whispered. I barely caught the words, the gentleness of her voice concealing. Even with this confession, I knew better than to reply. I knew better than to hope.

Chapter three

Voyager

We carried on as though nothing had happened. The kiss she left on my cheek came over me like a fever. And in the passing days, I believed it to be karma for calling her a disease. Though still infected, I thought she was divine. I didn't mean to say it aloud, I was just flushed with *want*. She brought out a side of me I didn't know existed. Concentrating was nearly impossible, I wanted to kiss her all the time. But once Solene and Michael became official, I knew I had to let this invention of love between us go. Everything then turned gloomy. *Everything* I touched grew into misery, watered by my own selfish reasons. Love wasn't the thing that could save me.

"The sex isn't the best part. It's that he really listens to me." Solene is talking to Sam and I, but I'm not really listening. I feel trapped by her charismatic chat. I wanted things to dull down already so this part wouldn't hurt as much. The part where I witness her be with somebody else. I can hardly stomach the thought of it. Solene married, mothering fat babies, becoming a housewife; I was spiraling.

"And to think, Michael wasn't even your type." Samantha said, completely smitten by the young couple.

"What is your type, exactly?" I asked, chiming in on the conversation for the first time.

Solene laughed, but her face didn't look amused.

"Why does it matter?" She said, looking at Samantha as they exchanged muffled giggles. It made my blood boil.

"I have to go home." I said, pushing up off the floor. We'd been sitting in the poetry aisle of the local bookstore for the past two hours, whispering about love and sex, and quite frankly I was done. I looked at Solene one last time but she refused to look up from a copy of *If not, winter*. Samantha waved goodbye, smiling apologetically.

I get it. You have a boyfriend. But I'm supposed to be your best friend. When do you ever make time for me? I deleted the text. I then type out *I knew you first, like really knew you*. I groaned and tossed my phone aside. We hadn't spoken since that day in the bookshop. I knew she was mad at me but I wasn't sure why. I was mad too. I wasn't going to be the first one to break the silence.

Interwoven in me is a girl and woman named coyote. I can't help but hunt the remnants of what desire I have left. I forget that I am animal. I forget that I am housed by fury. I forget that *I am*. But on a day where I'm on fire, on a fall day where it's hot in a way that suggests that this earth is *ending*, I come to realize that I don't feel alive when I'm not burning. When I'm not hurting, I feel shell-less. This body of bones is begging to break. It was the fifth day of not hearing from Solene and I wasn't sorry for the mess I made. Mad at each other, I knew in my anger I only found yearning. I bet I could still *want* her if she chose to stab me. *The blood would only bring us closer.* I found yearning in this frustration and so I touched myself and thought *Solene, don't hate me but yell if you need to*. And then when I finished, I'd reach for my phone and think to text her an apology. *Solene, I'm sorry. I'll give Michael a chance*. But what I type instead is *Solene, be inside me for more time than you're willing to give*. I even start touching myself while typing this out. I think of interrupting our feud to make love below the orange tree. We can fight after. Just to see her eat another orange. More than anything, let me taste the orange on her skin. I was lying in bed, journal on my chest, hand sliding down the front of my jeans when my phone buzzed. It was Solene. She was the first to break.

It's pretty shitty that you can't support my relationship with Michael when I've been there for you, always.

I put my phone back on the bedside, along with my journal and continued to touch myself. I'll reply with *You aren't there for me in ways that I want*. But that isn't fair. I could pick a fight by saying *Did you know Michael tried to finger me a couple years back while we watched a movie*? I was walking on eggshells between yearning and anger. I wanted to get back at her. I wanted to be the one who touched her, only if she asked. I closed my eyes and tried to keep my noises to myself as I felt my climax near. I could call her and let her hear me, I could hold the phone to my mouth and say her name. My thighs shook at the thought of her reaction. Would she feel instant heat between her legs, or would she hang up? I decided not to respond. It would feed the anger even more. I was winding her up.

When the pleasure died down and I was left outside the high I sought, I felt guilt. As if I were a dog who had been scorned, I retreated with my head down. I didn't like who I was after I touched myself. I showered. I wrote down the cons of being in love with someone who was not available. And I washed my sheets, twice. *Solene, I can't go out in the night and come back anew. The moon can't swallow this want. I hear the leaves crunching along to my footsteps and every thought matters because they are all about you, you, you.* I left my room, which I was hiding in, and decided to not panic when the sun showed itself brutally. I will panic when all is lost, but for now I can salvage this. I can pull out the dagger. Yet at this moment, it's lonely on the corner of Main Street.

It was the night of another party at Michael's house and I was dragged there by Samantha. Solene didn't acknowledge me, even though I changed my outfit four times, finally settling on something I've never worn before. I reached for a red solo cup and filled it halfway with tequila, sipping it thoughtlessly as I watched her dance with Samantha. I was already feeling tipsy by the time they both danced their way into my space, Samantha putting her hands on my waist.

"You look hot!" Samantha yelled. I watched the colored strobe lights wash over Solene as she stared right back at me. I put the brim of the cup to my mouth to hide the way I *wanted* to stare. "Are you two going to end this little feud?" Samantha grabbed both our hands and pressed

Solene into me. The scent of cinnamon made my stomach flutter.

"You didn't reply to my text."

"I'm sorry..."

"I can tell you don't like Michael." Solene said, twisting a finger in my hair. She was wasted, I could tell by the way she slurred and pushed up against me.

"I like Michael."

"Liar." She said.

"I'll try to do better." I finally said, downing the rest of my drink. My vision had become blurry. *Our anger* must've been part of my delusion.

"This is our song!" Solene said, asking me to dance by taking my hand. It was some sort of sick joke because I heard the lyrics *I thought that I was dreamin' when you said you love me* and for the slightest moment we froze in time. The lighting was dark red and I looked at her with a sultry, longing glance. She looked back, chest heaving from the pause in movement. We inched closer.

"Michael's looking for you!" Ronny shouted over the loud blare of the music. We locked eyes, for only a matter of seconds, which in return felt like centuries, and then she was turning away. Lost in the crowd.

It wasn't until later that evening, when I was nearly six drinks in, that I realized I was flirting with a girl named Phoebe. We had a couple classes together but that was the entire extent of our history. Now we were fumbling into a dark room, laughing about the ugly wallpaper as she turned on the light.

"You're really pretty." Phoebe said as I settled onto the bed, pushing back my hair to let it air out. I was feeling warm.

"I don't really do this..." I began.

"Which part?"

"All of it." I said, fanning myself. I was drunk, burning up, and there was a beautiful blonde girl in bed with me.

"You've never been with a girl before?"

"Never."

Suddenly Phoebe was close. She didn't smell of cinnamon but it was still nice, the way she felt soft and patient. I knew I was drunk and bound to make a mistake, but I still leaned in and put her mouth to mine. She hummed in approval, tasting of tequila and flavored lip gloss that reminded me of cherries. I closed my eyes and selfishly thought of Solene. I gasped as her name nearly slipped from my lips. Phoebe took that as encouragement, climbing on top of me. I had no idea what I was doing, but I put my hands up her back and kissed eagerly, insincere with the way I was picturing every inch of this body to be Solene's. I snapped out of it once I felt her undo my bra, blushing at the idea of it all. I must have always wanted this because I helped her remove the rest of my clothes in a hurry. A bit uncoordinated yet satisfied, I let out a moan when I felt her fingers push inside me. Afterwards, we lay side by side. I could still hear the music shaking the walls.

"Pass me my clothes." I said shyly, feeling exposed all

at once.

We got dressed in silence and it wasn't until I hooked my bra did I then hear the door begin to open.

"Oh...there you are." It was an overly drunk Solene, now standing in the doorway with a drink in hand. I threw my shirt on and pushed my hair out of my face. Phoebe was thankfully dressed, but looking thoroughly pleased. Her face was still flushed. "Can you get out?" Solene slurred, narrowing her eyes at Phoebe.

"Solene..."

"It's okay, I need another drink anyways." Phoebe said, sliding past Solene and disappearing down the dark hallway.

"What?" I said, once we were alone.

"Is she a friend?" Solene asked, her pupils were huge and she seemed somewhat angry.

"We just met."

"Hey..." Solene stepped in front of me. "I'm not a disease."

"I know you're not. I'm sorry."

"You can't say something like that and expect everything to be fine. You can't come into my life and expect..."

"Expect what?" I said, weary by the way she was swaying as if she might fall any second.

"Nothing." Solene closed her eyes and rubbed at her temple, I wanted to comfort her for whatever distress she was going through. I needed to be there for her. "Who was that girl, anyways?" Solene said, eyes narrowed again.

"Her name is Phoebe." I couldn't help but laugh.

"I'm your friend." She said, eyes swelling up with tears. I stifle my laughter, immediately pulling her into a hug. I was perhaps far too drunk to be of comfort.

"You're my best friend." I said, careful with the way I felt her melting into me. So lush and honeyed, this was everything I wanted. And even as I felt her lashes brush my collarbone, I knew she wouldn't remember anything in the morning.

"Come on, let's go back to the party." I said, helping her onto her feet because we somehow found ourselves on the bed.

"Ara..." She began, head gravitating to my shoulder. "There's so many things I need to say to you." She managed to lift her dizzying head, eyes locked on my mouth. I was willing to hear her out, hear everything she had to say, but then sobriety hit. It hit hard. I began to panic at my own drunken decisions. I wasn't going to let Solene make the same mistake.

"We can talk in the morning." I said, determined to go find Michael so he could take care of her. *I'll take care of you, I'll take care of you.* Solene frowned and laid back down. I reluctantly let go of her hand as she turned over, she'll probably be fast asleep in minutes. I slipped out of the party after telling Michael where Solene was, and walked home despite the heaviness I now felt with each step.

I was trying my best. I wrote about nature a lot. I

46

skimmed through every single book I owned and came to the conclusion that Anne Carson was right. *Humans in love are terrible.* And still my desire was as big and flowing as the sea. I just didn't know how to contain it. Nor did I know how to handle my bitterness, my hands balled into fists while I watched Solene and Michael kiss. It was her idea to have all our friends at the orange tree. Our sacred space. Solene is alone with me in every dream I have of her. Just *us* and a record shattering earthquake. We don't mind the ending of the world, just as long as we get to feel one another's touch. Now I can't remember the last time we spent a day alone together.

"Ara, Solene told me you met Phoebe." Michael said, placing his arm around Solene's waist. I looked at Solene with daggers. Solene looked away from me.

"Yeah, she's cool." I shrugged.

"I'll make sure to invite her next time we all hangout." Michael said, perking up. Solene was now the one with eyes like knives. Maybe in another life I'd be a man for Solene, if that's what she wanted. I'd be the boy with a dozen flowers, waiting at her doorstep.

I needed a break from this, from her. I needed to get away but there was nowhere to go. I was stuck. Nothing but the quiet murmur of the morning left to give me the peace I needed. Only left to be devoured by the afternoon, the only time of day when my *want* was unbearable. At night, I could at least have it be true. I would read poetry until I was sleepy, insatiable until I closed my eyes. Solene, tangled up with me in the warmest bed I've ever felt. I was no longer afraid when the apocalypse came. And by morning I sat up, always reaching for my journal. I wrote down *Our bodies, living vicariously through dreams. Dreams that you'll never know of. Our bodies, meant to withstand immense pain. We are the inflictors.* I never finish my train of thought, but through the haze I try my best to put it into words. Always falling short.

Today was a day where I felt spiritual, a sublime composure coming over me as I watched the orange tree imitate an oil painting. Solene was with me, of course. She was reading Dostoevsky. I was reading Mary Oliver. *With all these books I read and all these songs I play in your presence, can't you see I'm trying to get through to you? The wildness of this love sets us apart from other humans, Solene.*

"I can't read anymore." I announced once all the words on the page began to blur together.

"Me too." Solene said, closing the book and setting it aside. "What should we do?"

"I'm not sure." I frowned. It was now quiet, in the way you could hear a pin drop. Not even the wind made a sound, despite the breeze.

"Race you to the lake?" Solene said, pulling me up with her.

"It's too cold to swim."

"You're no fun."

We were still holding hands. I looked down and then at our discarded books and her ratty old blanket. I felt my

48

heart swell. We were alone.

"Okay." I agreed, dropping her hand in favor of cleaning up in a hurry to win the race.

Once at the lake I undressed, already shivering. It was late fall and the days were short. Solene dipped into the water so effortlessly, beckoning me to follow. I was tortured by the effect the sunset had on her skin. Golden hour happened because of her, she was radiance personified. Whether she be a myth or an actual wonder, the Gardens of Babylon couldn't compare. I'd like to think she was real, as real as my own flesh and blood that crooned whenever she walked into a room.

I dove in, gasping at the freezing temperature, my teeth immediately chattering. I swam to join her in the deep water, hoping the remainder of the sun would warm me.

"Solene..." I called out. She had disappeared. The water held still and then a sudden ripple, she emerged with a deep inhale. Solene was now tight against me, draping her arms around my shoulders. We were both breathing heavily, fighting to stay afloat.

"Hi." Solene smiled.

"Hi." She knew damn well what she was doing, she knew how I would bend into any shape for her, she knew she could ruin me.

"Sometimes I wish I could read your mind." Solene said.

"You can just ask." I said. The moon was revealing itself now, intertwining with the sun's last ray of beauty. I could count every freckle on her face. She looked at me with a solemn composure, eyes darting between my lips and eyes.

"Solene." *Don't do this. I wanted this. I mean, I can't breathe in a world where you don't exist. But please, don't do this. Not now.*

"Ara." She said it so matter of factly, I wanted to drown right then and there. And as sudden as it began, it ended with a splash and she was backstroking her way to the dock. I felt relieved. Or maybe I felt like dying. Either way, she could never be mine. Not with this greedy disposition that clouded my judgment. We dried off by laying out on the dock, my body covered in goosebumps. I closed my eyes and waited for her to speak first. *Say something Solene, say something to put me out of my misery.* Bearing some semblance to hope, I cursed myself at the stupidity. If she wanted to, she would. She would kiss me and burn alongside me, and we'd be Great Rome that turned to ash. We'd be a hurricane. A stampede. I was foolishly hoping, and rejecting and deciding, in that moment, to let *go.* No more borrowed time with a girl who unknowingly planted her roots. Roots of sadness and desperation, and a longing so wide philosophers and poets couldn't even measure its vastness. I made a home out of a body.

"Are you happy, Ara?" Solene said, swathed in moonlight. I took my time to absorb the question, really ponder it.

"I think so..."

"I don't believe you." She interrupted. Her presence

now had an anxious air to it.

"Solene, what do you want me to say?"

"I care about you. I want to know that you're alright. I see you. And some days, though better than some, I can feel it."

"Feel what?" I was becoming defensive.

"Feel your resentment for, I don't know...life. Sometimes you seem so happy and then you're not." When I didn't say anything, she continued. "Do you remember when I said I wanted to run away?"

"Yeah."

"I still think about it. Every time I think about you being trapped inside that house with your father. Or when I think about this town. We deserve better than this, Ara."

I didn't know what to say, her roots were invading my entire body. I felt wordlessly worried. I'd leave everything behind if it meant we could have the world at the tips of our fingers.

"Where would we go?" I finally said. Solene sat up, facing me with a look of anticipation.

"Anywhere. We could leave on a road trip with my grandmother. I know you think it's silly, but my grandmother doesn't have to know we're not coming back. We'll use her car, her money..."

"You sound insane."

"I have nothing here for me."

"You have Michael..."

"And you. But you'll come with, won't you?" She said

51

fiercely. I pinched the bridge of my nose. I had a headache.

"Think about it." She pleaded.

"Okay."

"Okay?"

"I'll think about it."

I knew it was losing battle. Solene says jump and I *jump*. I felt nervous in a way that felt like doom. Were we potentially doomed? I could only wish for a true poet's ending: We were born of clay, molding each other, only to be washed away in a sea of eagerness. I was ready to be eager with her, *for* her. I twined our pinkies together and she smiled at the subtle promise.

I was plotting our getaway, our jail break. We could drive and drive until this town was nothing but a speck in the rearview mirror. I tried to remember my wrath but there was only silence. I felt alive. Within the silence, I could hear my heartbeat. It was a peaceful lull. Within the silence, I was shown clarity. Although the perforation of my lungs did not vanish so easily, I was learning to love. To cry. To eat. To live. Or maybe I was just learning to nestle into another soul so obsessively that I interpreted their heartbeat to be my own.

There were a lot of things we did not talk about. Solene walking in on me and Phoebe. Solene staring at my mouth. Solene saying *this is our song*. We did not talk about these things because perhaps it was all in my mind. I was desperately imaginative in order to survive.

"Michael and I are fighting."

I didn't want to talk. I wanted to continue staring at my bedroom ceiling.

"Fighting about what?" I said.

"He's mad because I didn't sleep with him last night. I was tired."

"He should respect your boundaries. What a stupid thing to be mad about..."

"Ara, he's my boyfriend. Maybe he's allowed to..."

"Don't defend him." I snapped. "I know he's the first person you've ever slept with but it's not meant to be like this."

"To be like what?"

"To be so complicated. You shouldn't feel sorry for not giving him sex. You're supposed to want it too." I sighed, finally looking over to her as she stared back contemplatively.

"Thank you." Solene murmured. Putting her arm around me, she buried her face into my neck and inhaled. I stiffened but didn't pull back. She was someone I had to have. In any way. A friend. A lover. I put my arms around her and almost kissed the top of her head. I almost gave in and then she was sitting up, wiping away a tear.

"I'll kick his ass."

"Ara, it's fine." Solene laughed.

"It's not." None of this was fine. Michael was not known for his good intentions.

"I'll talk to him." Solene said.

Turn me on and I'll give in.

"Okay." I said.

Touch me if you want to and I'll never complain again.

"You're a good friend." Solene said, gripping my hand. I almost took it as a sign as I leaned in. Her eyes were back on my mouth. We kiss and then I die. We kiss and then I'm an evaporated planet. I realized I was too close to her and daydreaming. I sat back and Solene stared at me, amused. We'll never kiss and I'll never die as beautifully as a shooting star.

"Ara..."

"We should go on a bike ride..."

"Ara..." Solene began but she never finished because her eyes were on my mouth and it was like she couldn't concentrate. "I should get home. My grandmother wanted help with dinner."

"Oh... Okay." I said and then we were hugging goodbye, tight yet softly. I closed my eyes and felt my desperation fill my mouth like venom. Solene held me close and her heartbeat, pounding, configured to mine. I knew she could feel me shaking.

"See you tomorrow?" I asked.

"Yeah." And then she was letting me go, but not before gliding the bridge of her nose across my cheekbone. *Solene, be easy on me. Take me apart slowly.*

"Solene..." I said, timidly.

And then her phone began to buzz. Her skin was off mine in a flurry.

"It's Michael." Solene looked at me. I was still daydreaming, wasn't I?

"Have a good night." I said, shuffling her off the bed. "Go and fix things with Michael. Make dinner with Vinos. I'll see you later."

"Okay."

You should have kissed me right here, in this bed.

She left out the front door and I went to go shower. I was feeling used up and restless. I scrubbed my body, like I always do, until it was red as if I was ridding traces of her. I knew it was for the better, not to get involved. But God, did I want to. Buzzards swarming a deer on the roadside. A person who sees water while stranded in the desert. Bees on a newly bloomed flower. A mirage. A funeral. I was mourning someone who was still alive. I was longing, deep and smoldering. My dreams that night were deformed and sensual. I knew no other way out.

We didn't speak of running away since that day on the dock. Silence on her end hardly gave me peace. I was threatened by it. That's when I heard a knock at the door, my heart racing to see if it was Solene. It was Samantha.

"I thought we could hangout." She said, walking in through the door while I held it open. I tried to hide my disappointment. I was greedy with anticipation. *Are we really doing this? Are we running away?*

"How are you?" Samantha asked once we were in my room.

"I'm good."

"And your father?"

"The same."

She frowned.

"Oh... I have something to tell you!" She exclaimed as something dawned on her. "Solene broke up with Michael."

I blinked.

"Why?" It was the only word I could muster up.

"I don't know. She doesn't seem too torn over it, though."

I had to find her. I got up from my bed, pacing around, only to see Samantha staring at me wide eyed.

"Ara, are you okay?"

"Yeah, sorry." I sat back down.

Maybe, slowly but surely, our plan to run away was falling into place. Solene was chipping away at her current life to make room for her new one. Maybe that day on my bed led to this? Maybe this yearning was for something, not nothing. I wanted Samantha to leave so I could pack my bags. My phone buzzed. It was a single text from Solene that read

Meet me at the orange tree.

Chapter four

These hands, if not gods

There were very few things I would beg for in this lifetime. Her *mouth*, one of the things I'd righteously beg for. Although I would receive no answer. For that, I will never speak again. So on this day in the field, beneath the orange tree, was something out of dreams. Something I in fact would have never dreamed of because the human mind is not capable of such imagination. Solene watched as I got off my bike, bemused. I must've looked frantic by the way I threw it down and collapsed onto her ratty blanket. I looked around, cautiously.

"You two broke up?" I didn't mean to say it so callously but I was on the brink of elation.

"Yes." She nodded.

"Just like that?"

"Just like that." Solene insisted.

"And your grandmother? Have you told her about the road trip?"

"Ara…" Solene gave me a look that I knew very well.

"Oh." I felt childish. "This was your idea, you know. This was your idea and I didn't even want to do it in the first place. Now you go and change your mind…" I was crying now, hardly noticeable as the tears pricked my eyes, but I knew she could tell. Michael was gone. I had her all to myself. How was that not enough? Did I really ever have her to begin with?

"Ara, it's okay. We'll figure something out. You'll be eighteen by the end of the summer and you can move out of your father's house. It'll be okay."

"It won't be okay, Solene. Nothing is okay." I said. "I called you a disease. I hear you quote Siken to me. You touch me in ways that has me spinning. When you're drunk, you say things..."

"What do I say?" Solene said, as if urging me to push her buttons.

"Do you remember that night at Michael's party?"

"Barely." She looked pale at my sudden outburst.

"I slept with that girl and you walked in and confused me even more by acting jealous. But God, Solene, if it's all in my head please tell me." I said, desperately.

Solene picked up an orange beside her and began to study it. I wanted to leave, I was ready to leave, but then she was handing the orange over to me like a truce. I had this colossal urge to deny it. I wanted her to hurt in the same way I've been hurting since summer. I stood my ground.

"I *was* jealous, Ara." She said, beginning to peel the orange, concentrating solely on the orange. Ripping apart the fruit, she got up onto her knees and offered the bare piece, fingers dripping. After careful consideration, I leaned in, petrified. Solene, her hazel hair in that schoolyard. Solene, her apocalyptic shaped mouth. Solene, *you're ruining my life*. Solene, Solene. Solene. A throbbing pulse took over my lungs. This prominent feeling was now inescapable.

Solene, an *inescapable* angelic being. *My Solene.* Her thumb and pointer finger entered my mouth, the sweetness of the orange juices encompassing my taste buds. I sucked, softly. Reluctantly letting her fingers go, I put a hand on both sides of her face. She closed her eyes. I gently traced her lips with the tip of my tongue as if her mouth might crumble from my touch. It's sensual and earth shattering. Her lips are being carved by me and I find it to be the most intimate moment of my life.

"Ara..." She moaned against my mouth. Taking the orange from her now tight fist, I smeared it across her chest so I could lap up each streak of moisture. I feel her entire body vibrate. *Pinch me.*

"Is this okay?" I asked, as she began to run her hands through my hair. She nodded, vigorously. I travel downward, the juices of the orange following. When I reach her thighs, I look up to see if I've overstepped. Her face was magic, in that moment she was holy and *magic* and all that defied truth. *Don't stop*, her eyes said it first. Solene spreads her legs and my vision blurs as I try to unbutton her shorts in a hurry. *Hurry* as in, I've waited my whole life for this. *Let me taste you.* My unholy mouth meets her altar and her hands tighten in my hair. The darkness of the field is approaching, the crickets are booming from each direction. Aside from nature, I hear a cozy hum. It was Solene saying my name, over and over, like a prayer. Sticky and delirious, I roll onto my back and gasp for air. She was now the one to climb on top, pressing our foreheads together.

"Ara."

"I know." I said, kissing her with so much abandon I nearly faint. So much time was wasted.

"I've wanted this for so long." Solene said.

I smiled and gave her a small kiss. It was reassurance for the culpability we both must've felt, for taking too long to get *here*. *Here* on this earth, together, where the moon and tide existed. The wind picked up and we shuddered in each other's arms. It was time to go but neither of us was willing to suggest it. Days could pass and so could the seasons, and I'd still bury myself in her. No matter how cold or wet, sultry or blazing, I'd be by her side to relish in her martyrdom for eternity.

"Kiss me some more." Solene said. We were just two girls, in a field, at night, who hours later were unaware of these habits we'd be creating, hopefully, for the rest of our lives. I kiss her slowly, savoring the taste of orange and saliva and the sweat that broke out on her upper lip. The night goes on like this: Her mouth meets mine and we only come up for air when it's necessary. Beneath her tongue, there is a poem and I find it every time.

I woke up shivering from the cold morning air, partly undressed with Solene cuddled into me. I felt peace for a brief moment until it hit me. *We fell asleep.* I looked at my phone and saw the time, six a.m. and four missed calls from my father.

"Shit. Solene. Get up." I said, shaking her awake. I

suddenly felt exposed, searching in the dark for my shirt. I buttoned my shorts back up.

"What?" She mumbled.

"We fell asleep. Fuck, your grandma has probably reported you missing."

"Shit!" Solene said, eyes flying open.

"Let me help you." I said, gathering her clothes.

"Don't, Ara. Just don't." She snapped, taking her clothes from my hand. Before I could comprehend what just happened, she was already dressed and taking off on her bike. I was now left in the field, orange peels strewn around me, remembering the way she stored her fingers inside me. I felt sick at the sudden thought of her regretting this. I pictured my mother standing before me, holding her book as she said, "*And if your eye causes you to stumble, pluck it out. It is better for you to enter the kingdom of God with one eye than to have two eyes and be thrown into hell.*" If it was a mistake, Solene, I'll tear out my eyes. I will.

Back at home, I snuck into the bathroom and went into the shower. Washing away all the oranges and *her*, I broke down crying. *The end of you and I is approaching, isn't it, isn't it* my heart thrummed.

A week passes by and Solene is gone. Gone from this Earth, so it seems. And I am gone from my mind. There are days where I see her from afar and my dreams become more frightening by the minute. Afraid to sleep, afraid to breathe, I hover my finger over her name in my phone and I almost call. The very bottom of this hole is bitter and lonely. I dig myself deeper.

"You're not sick." My father said, standing in my doorway. He was sober which meant he chose to act like a father. I resented it.

"I have a fever." I said, removing the pillow I was using to smother myself.

"It's been seven days, kiddo. Your principal said you're going to fall behind."

"I don't care."

"Ara..."

"Dad, please."

"You're going back tomorrow." He said, firmly. I put the pillow over my face again.

The yearning before the night at the orange tree seemed bearable. The yearning now was unthinkable; a bellyache that never subsided. It was something that left a bad taste in my mouth, that entered my lungs and never escaped. The *quiet* that came after the sex was like a rustling of leaves. Now I am just left with the quiet. And I swore I was not cursed with a blank heart, I just had nothing left to say.

"Get out of bed." Samantha said, yanking off my bed sheet that was wrapped around me.

"Go away." I whined. I felt like my stomach had solidified into cement.

"I know you and Solene had a falling out, but that's no reason to brood."

"Leave me alone."

"Don't be a bitch."

"I can't help it." I said.

"I'm not going to let you push me away." Samantha said, "You have no one else."

"Have you talked to her?" I asked, tentatively. I couldn't say her name out loud.

"Yeah. Are you going to tell me what happened?" Samantha sat down at the edge of the mattress. "Do I have to kick her ass?"

"Are you bisexual?" I said.

"I guess so. Why?"

"Sam... Something is wrong with me. I'm not gay...at least I don't think I am. But..." I let everything instantly spill out of me. "Me and Solene slept together."

There was a long pause when suddenly Samantha burst into a fit of laughter. I propped myself up on my elbows and glared at her. She covered her mouth with her hand.

"Holy shit!" She said, "I knew it!"

"Shut up!"

"Ara..."

"No, don't say anything. There's nothing you can say that will fix me."

"You think you need fixing?" When I didn't answer, she continued. "You slept with a girl, so fucking what."

"It's not just that." I inhaled sharply. "It's everything. My mother's dead, my father's probably next. I can't breathe most days."

"Have you told anyone else how you feel?" Samantha's humor evaporated as her brows knitted together with concern.

"I've talked to Solene about it."

"Forget her. I'm here now."

The idea of forgetting Solene terrified me.

The violent past I carry could very well be my future. What if the troubles my mother had passed down to me? I was incubated in grief from the very beginning. I remember her first attempt, with the blood on the bathroom floor as she stood over the sink. It comes in waves, visions of her. Her white nightgown, she sang me a lullaby. My father and his happiness, he thought his love was enough to save her. Not too long after, I found my mother in bed in her own puddle of vomit, she had overdosed. The note she left was short and simple. It didn't mention me or my father. To this day, I think that's what truly broke him. Despite his neglect in the long run, I looked for my own way to cope. The first thing being religion, to be closer to my mother. She believed. My father was an atheist. So I went to seek God to spite him. Turns out I imagined God to be a hateful man, one who would punish any woman at the snap of his fingers. It took me years to come to terms with this, that I was being *punished* for being a woman. I bled and cramped, I kicked and screamed, and still, I was bottled up with rage.

I dreamt of Solene that night, the first dream in a long

time where we were familiar with one another. Familiar enough I could feel her breathe into my mouth. *Your lungs, an extension of mine.* We were breathing together, synced by chemistry. I said, "*I was born hungry for you.*" And then I was awake, my lungs pounding in my ribcage. My own ascension into madness was happening and I am a witness. I am a witness to the temper I maintain, only tending to the fire that is burning me alive. I stoke it myself.

"I miss her."

"I think we should stop talking about *her*." Samantha insisted. We were in my bedroom, doing homework. I was back in school, trying my best to catch up. I saw her in class today. It was as if I was invisible. It was just as painful as I imagined the encounter to be.

"Has she mentioned me yet?"

Samantha sighed. "Fine, let's talk about it. No, she hasn't said anything." I looked at Samantha as she scooted closer. "Do you love her?"

"Yes."

"I'm sorry, Ara." Samantha's empathy was soothing.

"I wish I didn't." I said, resting my head on Samantha's shoulder.

My love for Solene was an imposition. What did that make me to her? Did she also carry me around like a burden, a wicked cross to bear?

"Everything will be alright." Samantha said. I wanted to believe her. I really did.

I kissed her hard in my nightmares. And when she kissed me back, I should've walked away right then and there. But every ounce of her craze fed into me like an IV. *Somehow you got into my veins. Somehow my very marrow wants you.*

When I received a letter from my university of choice in the mail that morning, I tore into it. The rejection was in the first sentence. I had no reaction but to set it on the counter and walk away. I didn't care if my father saw it. And when he came into my room with the letter in hand, I wasn't afraid.

"It's okay, Ara. It's not the end of the world."

"I'm not sure I want to go to college."

"You're smart and talented." He wasn't drunk, just tipsy. It was the stage where he became solicitous.

"Can we talk about something else?"

"Are you okay?" He sounded genuinely concerned. He has watched me throw away every meal after taking one bite, he has watched me lay in bed for hours on end, he has even heard me cry in the bathroom as I tried to do my makeup. I loathed him for caring.

"You're still a kid. You're still too young to know it gets better."

His reassurance almost felt sincere. I would've believed if it hadn't been for the fact it's been years since my mother passed and *still*, my father chose to bury himself with her.

I went to bed that night upset. I deserved more than this. If I could give myself the world, intact, then I would. No more dead birds falling from the sky, no more water rising above the mountains, just a soft reckoning for the ones who have suffered most. My phone then lit up on my bedside table, I reached over and squinted at the brightness. It was Samantha.

I don't mean to say this to hurt but to help you. Solene kissed some guy at a party tonight. I put my phone to my chest and blinked several times before reading it again. And just like that, she was dead to me. Was it that easy? Could I really just use hate to replace several months of love I had for her? I balled up into the fetal position, mind racing. I texted Samantha back. *Glad she's moving on.*

"Where's your girlfriend?" I heard a familiar voice say. I looked up from my book to find Phoebe standing in front of me in the schoolyard.

"What girlfriend?" I stammered, looking around to make sure no one heard her.

"That girl, who walked in on us at the party." Phoebe laughed.

"She's not my girlfriend." I said.

"So why haven't you texted me?" She said, feigning a frown.

"You didn't give me your number."

"Do you want to go out with me tonight?" Phoebe asked. I glanced around again, observing the schoolyard. I

67

was seeking out Solene as if I could make her jealous, as if I even mattered to her. Although dead to me, I still had this *need* to let her know I was moving on, too.

"Yeah, I'll go out with you." I smiled. The bell rang to signify the end of lunch. I put my journal into my bag and slung it over my shoulder. Without hesitation, I held out my phone and she smiled at the wordless interaction. I watched as she put in her number, afraid she could sense just how naive I really was.

"See you later, Ara." Phoebe said, handing back my phone. I waved goodbye and headed in the direction of English class. Had Solene not known I was ready to surrender to her? Now it was too late, our time was diminished to a pulp. And in that instance, I attempted to unabashedly accept that I was going out with the girl who was openly lesbian. I began to stress what I should wear, where would we go? Surely not in public, I wasn't ready. Did she think we'd go out to some fancy dinner, holding hands from across the table? My nerves felt agitated. I was on the brink of panic. I had to find Samantha. Luckily we had class together, so I caught up to her before she entered the room.

"Sam, I need to talk to you."

"Is this about my text? I'm sorry for..."

"No, no, it's about Phoebe Collins."

"What about her?"

"She asked me out..." I whispered. "Like on a date."

Samantha blinked and then broke out into a smile. I didn't smile in return, I stared back tight lipped.

"That's a good thing, right?" Samantha said. "If you're second guessing because of Solene..."

"I'm second guessing because I'm confused, Sam."

"Everything will be alright." She said, reassuringly. The second bell rang so our conversation was cut short. I entered class feeling as if the ground might shift, like it would crumble if I took one wrong step. The precariousness I felt was neither in reference to Solene or her absence, rather the reality was I had slept with two girls and the world did not end.

Phoebe picked me up in her car in the evening. I slipped into the front seat, smoothing out the creases on my short skirt I chose to wear last minute. She ogled me smugly, her confidence was something worth envying.

"I was thinking we'd go up the canyon. I have a spot that overlooks the valley." Phoebe said, pulling out the driveway.

"Sounds good." I said.

The drive was nice, music lulled me to relaxation. We talked about school, friends, and books. Turns out Phoebe was an avid reader. I was at complete ease by the time we got to the lookout. Phoebe parked her car, turning the radio up. I felt nervous, watching as she applied chapstick in the rearview mirror.

"You're staring." Phoebe said, turning to face me, teeth gleaming.

"No I'm not." I said, looking down at my hands.

"I don't mind." She said, taking her seatbelt off to

edge closer. I peered back at her. The way she tucked her hair behind her ears to reveal her jawline was my invitation to lean in. We kissed for a while, making our way into the backseat, removing each other's clothes as if it was ritual. Not too long after, I felt a creeping sensation in the pit of my stomach. It was the taste of oranges, the scent of cinnamon, it was the way Phoebe's body pressed into mine and I wished for it to stop. It was Solene. She was the sensation that nagged at parts of me when I was trying my best to forget about her. She was the ceremonious hum throughout my very core. To my embarrassment I began to cry. Phoebe pulled away with a look of concern.

"I think I've made a mistake." I whispered.

"What do you mean?"

"Solene, the one who walked in on us. She wasn't my girlfriend. But she is someone I have feelings for. More than feelings, I'm in love with her."

"What happened?"

"We had sex." I said. "Now she won't talk to me."

"Have you tried talking to her?"

"No." I paused. "She said she was straight."

"And do you think that's true?"

"I don't even know if *I'm* gay." I said.

"I came out to my parents when I was thirteen years old." Phoebe said, "And I came out because I was, without a doubt, gay. It doesn't come as clear to everyone as it did to me. But there's a reason you feel so trapped, there's a reason you feel this confused."

"And a reason I feel so ashamed." I said, reaching for my shirt on the floor of the car. I couldn't bear to look at her. "I want to hate her. But I can't."

"Be easy on yourself. Be easy on her. If you're scared, she's just as scared."

"I'm sorry." I said, still weeping. "I didn't mean for the date to go this way."

"Close your eyes." Phoebe said.

"Why?"

"Just close your eyes."

I closed my eyes as her hands framed my face.

"Now, when I kiss you, just ask yourself how it feels." Phoebe instructed, calmly. Before I could say anything, her lips were against mine, her tongue pushing into my mouth. It was slow, sensual, and the flutter in my stomach was anything but shame. I was safe and sound and in all my worry I was suddenly filled with a sense of clarity. Clarity for all the girls I have desired. And Solene, this *desire*, unmatched. I opened my eyes and Phoebe pulled away. *It feels right.*

I asked to borrow my father's car the next day so I could drive to the ocean. The ocean is what my mother gave to me. She'd take me to the water and tell me about the creatures below. She'd tell me to give all my troubles to the water and let the tide carry it away. This is what I liked to remember most; my mother standing on the beach in a sundress, laughing miraculously as my father picked her up and carried her into the waves to throw her in. The drive to the ocean was long and thrilling. I kept the windows rolled down, the air slightly chilly, while my favorite songs drifted through the speakers. I parked the car on the side of the road once I was at the first beach I spotted. Traveling down the grassy hill, I noticed the beach was vacant. I sat down in the sand and looked at the water. I didn't know exactly why I was here or what I wanted from the ocean this time. Perhaps I wanted to go into the water and let it swallow me whole. *Was I gay? Did I want Solene? Did I believe in God?* I closed my eyes and felt the wind sweep my hair from side to side. *God, if I really am gay let me feel good. If I'm straight, let me wake up with a desire for a husband.* I opened my eyes and shook my head. Who was I talking to? Myself? Yet, I liked how the questions left my mind and went in the air. I looked around to see if I was truly alone. This time I spoke out loud. "God, you either accept me now or make me straight by tomorrow morning." Visions of my mother raced past me. Visions of Solene forged through me. I closed my eyes once more to let the tears stream down my face. I was crying because I was consumed with a feeling of acceptance. Not by God, but *acceptance of myself.*

The day after my revelation, the earth began to shake. And not just a slight tremble or a misstep on my part, but an actual shaking that instilled fear in those around me. When the shaking came to a halt, everyone began to check on one another. Some plants from nearby shelves were smashed on the floor, dirt scattered about, but no other damage was inflicted. I stuffed my journal into my bag and ran out of the coffee shop. *The world is ending and all I want is you, Solene.*

It was a 5.7 magnitude earthquake that struck the town. Solene was nowhere to be found. I searched all our favorite spots, desperate to be with her. Whether it be just as friends or lovers, I needed her close. *I'll go easy on her*, a promise I gave to Phoebe. I'll tell her just how much she means to me, I'll spend the rest of my life making up for lost time. The world nearly ended today, she must feel the same. She must be searching just as frantically. By evening, I had given up finding her. Pushing my bike in defeat, I promised myself this wasn't the end. *This end* would never come close to the actual one. No amount of breaking bones could ever come close. I didn't want to go home so I sat on a curb and removed my journal from my bag. I had little light left but I squinted at the page and began to write. *This thing in me is primal. Tangled in my organs, I can only dream of having you when the apocalypse is upon us. I can only have you when disaster strikes. Why can't I have you calmly? Calm does not run in my blood. Maybe a stillness. But never a calm that takes the form of patience. My yearning can never be patient for it wants you like an animal who sniffs out fear.* I closed my journal and decided it was time to go home to an unpredictable environment. I was still far away, past curfew, and *missing her*. But I did not let it deter me from finding Solene tomorrow or the next day or the next. Eventually I rounded the corner in my neighborhood with my head down.

"Ara." I heard her voice like an electric shock.

That's when I spotted *her*. All my self-confidence came back, my cravings hit me like a train. Sitting on my front porch was Solene. She was riveting. A force of nature. I was willing to give up my body as a confession, right then and there.

"Hi." I said, breathless from my long journey.

"Hi." She said, just as breathless. "Can I come in?"

I led us into the dark house, my father was probably away at some bar. I didn't bother turning any of the lights on, eager to get to my room. Eager to hear what she had to say.

Once in my room, before I could say anything, she collapsed into my arms, hands quivering.

"In Iraq, the bombs heard from my bedroom would make the walls shake." She began. "Today, when the earthquake happened, it was like I was back there. I looked for you as I fell to the ground. I looked for you because you're my safe place. I trust you with my life. But you weren't there and I realized there's no point if you aren't around."

Solene was *my* safe place, one that I found holy.

"I am nothing without you. Please Ara, forgive me."

I took her into my arms and kissed her hair. *Nothing* in this world could take her from me. We slept in my bed that night, fully clothed, yet fully immersed within each other. I stirred awake, nervous to find that she had disappeared again. Instead, she was still here, a part of me. The familiar scent of cinnamon brought me down to earth.

"Morning." She whispered against my cheek. I inhaled, twining our hands together.

"What time is it?"

"Just about seven. We should be getting to school."

I felt shy as I went to take my pajamas off, picking up a discarded bra on the floor. That's when I felt her hands on my back. I froze. She began to adjust my bra straps, kissing the nape of my neck. I knew she felt my entire body vibrate, but I was not embarrassed because she too shook against me, breath quickening. I turned around, looking at her mouth eagerly, she leaned in as I closed my eyes. Her lips began at my jawline, working their way up until she reached my eyelids. I couldn't help but moan softly, crumbling in her arms like wet clay. That's when I felt her tongue push inside. My knees almost gave out.

"We should..." I couldn't gather my thoughts. "We have school."

"Can I say something?"

"You don't need my permission."

"Ara, after we slept together...no matter how much I wanted to, I was afraid. I've never done this before. I grew up believing this was immoral. They threw people like me off buildings in my country. I believed if I ever gave in, I'd go to hell." She was crying now.

"I'm afraid too." I said. She nodded, drawing me in. We stood like this for quite some time as the morning light crept through the blinds.

It was as if no time had passed at all. Continuing on

together in this arcadia we discovered, my everyday sorrow turned dormant. With so much lost time to make up for, it was a surprise to find out how nervous we both were. Nervous to lose control, or perhaps apprehensive to lose ourselves. Our intimacy wavered. Most days were normal, our friendship platonic. I was just lucky enough to have known what she felt like. Her skin was wrapped in wool, her limbs radiant with femininity. I was devoted to her, like wolves to the moon.

"What's going on in there?" Solene said, rubbing my ankle with her thumb.

"Going on in where?"

"Your mind. What are you thinking about?"

"You."

Solene turned rosy, glancing down at the grass. We were back at the orange tree. It had been our first time here since *that night*.

"Sorry." I murmured.

"Why?"

"I don't want to overstep."

"You've seen me naked." Solene said, innocently.

I now was the one who was red.

"Okay," I paused. "I think about you every waking minute, Solene."

"I think about you too, Ara."

I was dying to tell her every thought I've ever had, down to the very one of *I'll rename myself for you, just so you know how domesticated I can be*. I wanted to hear the same from her, that we were both willing to bend into any shape for one another.

That's when I inched closer, wilting into her touch. We kissed briefly. For days I had interpreted her chaste attempt at boundaries as regret. The kiss was proof enough that all we needed was more time. More time to get *this* right.

"Tell me you want this." I said, brushing my lips against hers. I didn't mean for it to sound like I was begging, but I was aware of my broken cadence; the torment peeking through like light in a cave.

"I want you." She replied, turning the kiss into something eager. I took that as a sign to start removing my shirt. She stopped me quickly.

"Not here." She laughed. When I made a face, she kissed me once more and said, "My grandmother will be gone until the evening. We'll have the place to ourselves."

Back at Solene's, we walked side by side, calves brushing. She locked the door once we stepped into her room. My throat felt tight. She led me over to the bed, sitting me down.

"What if you leave again?" I said, fidgeting with my hands.

"I won't."

"There's no guarantee..."

"How can I earn back your trust?" She asked.

I stared at her like a deer in headlights.

"Ara, please. Say something."

In response, I climbed into her lap and undid the

zipper of her sweater. She laid back, bringing me with, feeling the length of her body pressed against mine. After removing all our clothes in a tranquil state, I slid my hand up her spine. We were still learning, but I was enthralled with how well we already knew each other's bodies. Slipping my hand between her legs, I felt her warmth.

Afterwards, as we lay beneath her sheets, I recalled a line from a Yuknavitch novel. *We met our wounds in each other's bodies.* I never spoke it out loud, but I knew deep down, that day, nothing would ever be the same. Exposed like a nerve, I was still rationalizing the fact we were built this way. Built to worship, have faith, and still overcome the pain inflicted within our short existence. Our wounds were now molded into one. I felt closer to heaven than I ever thought possible.

Chapter five

Cutthroat

My mother raised me to starve. Still to this day, I hear her voice in my head whenever I indulge. I used to hide my wrappers and sneak handfuls of chips into my room late at night, ashamed of how I would tear away at meat at the dinner table. Only to feel possessed to throw it up hours later. *My beautiful thin daughter* she would exclaim. I swear I did it because it seemed to be the only thing that made her happy. Even months before she died, she gifted me a book called *the 17 day diet*. I was only ten. I read every word, clinging to the delusion that I was the perfect daughter, always abiding by her rules. I could never resent her for it, she was ill. But sometimes, as I was cramming food into my mouth after a day of fasting, I couldn't help myself to think I was the reason she killed herself. It began after I was born, my father said. Postpartum psychosis. Not too long after she was diagnosed with bipolar and depression, refusing to take medication because she said it made her numb. I often thought of what my mother's life must've been like before she had me. She was gorgeous in photos, long jet black hair and fair skin, but the woman I knew had hollowed cheeks and dark rings under her eyes. My father told me she'd stand by my cradle and stare blankly as I cried all night long. I didn't stand a chance from the moment I left *her* womb. I never stood a chance as I became a daughter, never enduring the reconfiguration of her desire to be *my mother*.

To be female meant to be left scorched. Girlhood, pressurized in one giant patriarchal cooker; my mother and I had more in common than I'd initially thought. My father, though devoted, was never home due to work, gone days on end. Which ultimately led to my mother's symptoms to fall beneath his radar. It wasn't until he came home to rotten milk on the counter and a sobbing wife, did he then understand the gravity of the situation. She begged him to take me before she did something she'd regret.

I don't hate her. I don't feel bitter. But I still tell myself to only have fruit on odd days, saltine crackers on even ones. I still see *it was the only way out* scrawled in her spidery handwriting on a crumpled piece of paper. All I feel is guilt. I'm sure my father blames me too. I could feel his blame from across the room as I watched him drink. It was two in the afternoon, he was complaining that he needed something from the store. I knew it was because he was out of liquor. But I also knew he was in no state to drive. He grabbed his keys, making his way out the front door.

"Dad, stop." I pleaded, following him down the front porch steps.

"Ara, go back inside." He grumbled, walking unsteadily.

"Please dad, please don't drive." I said, reaching for his keys. He stared blankly at me. We never spoke out loud about his drinking. We never acknowledged anything.

"I'm fine to drive. Go back inside." He said, his voice

raising. I looked over to our neighbor, Larry, who was standing in his yard, pretending not to watch.

"If you get in that car, I'll call the cops." I whispered, trying not to make a scene.

My father stared at me with so much disdain, for a second I thought he was going to hit me. Instead he stormed back into the house, leaving me behind as I stood there visibly shaking. Larry, who has called the cops on my father in the past, was now staring with a look of sympathy. I realized at that moment I couldn't go back inside, fearful of what my father would say in the four walls of our home. I also couldn't leave because I knew he'd get in the car as soon as I was gone. So I sat on the front porch, for hours, mindlessly scrolling on my phone.

When I assumed the coast was clear, I went back inside. My father was standing in the living room, as if he'd been waiting for me.

"Ara, I'm sorry." He said. His sober tone was caring.

I stood there, not knowing what to say.

"I'm awful. I'm so sorry." He repeated, now visibly weeping.

"Don't cry, dad." My voice was barely above a whisper.

"Your mother would hate me for how I treat you."

My father never mentioned my mother. I felt conflicted, still cautious of his intentions. He was rarely sober, but when he was he hardly spoke. This was new to me, it was like having a glimpse of *my* father back.

"You need help." I said.

He nodded, stepping closer. I flinched. That's when he pulled me into a tight hug, putting his hand to the back of my head. I closed my eyes and felt nurtured for the first time in years.

Not long after my father went to bed, I called Solene, asking if she could sneak out and come see me. I was seeking more comfort and suddenly optimistic in every aspect of my life. She agreed and said she would be over in twenty minutes. I sat on my bed, patiently, anxious to see her. Once she arrived we crept down the hallway, slowly closing my bedroom door as she took my hand and kissed each fingertip.

"How are you?" She asked, sensing my apprehension.

"It's been a long day." I sighed, laying down as she followed suit. I stared at the ceiling for quite some time, feeling her twine our feet together. I turned on my side and kissed her. We kept quiet as we undressed. We kept quiet as we merged together. We even kept quiet as our movement became vigorous, only gently making noises in each other's ears. For only *us* to hear, for only *us* to experience.

"Do you believe in God?"

It was the next day, the early morning light emitting through the window. Lying on my stomach, I waited for her answer.

"Sometimes." Solene said, tracing shapes onto my skin. "Like right now, the way the sun is dancing across your back, I can't help but believe in something."

I hid my face in the pillow, smiling. There was no such thing, no angels or miracles. Yet I knew what she meant. Her touch felt like a religion. But I wanted to say *how could you after all that has happened? After all that you've been through?* It wasn't my place to question someone else's way to fend for themselves. Because that's what a *God* did, create destruction and leave you to clean it up.

"Do you believe in God, Ara?"

"No." I said, as if I was disappointed. I could tell her how I used to pray to God every night to make my mother well. I could say my fear of God was debilitating. I was lost because so many others spoke of faith as a compass. It was just me and only me.

We got ready for school in a hurry. She wore *my* clothes and I felt deliriously in love. It wasn't until I went to open my door, did she then take my hand with a look of concern.

"At school, you know we can't be like this, we can't be *us*." Solene said.

"I know."

She may never know how many times I had to stop myself from touching her when we were just friends. Solene then smiled, kissing me one last time before we left.

Once outside, headed to the driveway where our bikes sat, I saw Larry begin to approach me. Solene, utterly confused, looked at me and then at Larry.

"Your father came over last night, asking if I had any liquor."

My heart sank.

"What time?"

"Maybe around midnight. I was asleep when I heard him knocking."

"I'm sorry, it won't happen again."

"It's not a problem. I'm just concerned." Larry said, waving his hand like my father's wrongdoings were nothing but a minor inconvenience.

"I'm going to be late for school." I said, kicking up my bike stand. When we were out of the neighborhood, I stopped pedaling and nearly collapsed. Solene was right there, instantly, telling me to breathe. I hated to hope, I hated *myself* for hoping.

"I have to leave, I have to get out of this town." I said, anguished.

"I know." Solene said.

"Whether you come or not, I'm leaving."

"We better get to school." Solene murmured.

I can feel myself becoming something grotesque, sewn together with parts I no longer recognized.

School that day was long and uneventful. I went through the motions, hardly seeing what was in front of me. The despair I was experiencing emitted from me in ways I could not control, therefore Solene would not stop asking if I was okay.

"Just drop it." I said to her as Samantha came to take her place at the table in the schoolyard.

"You two finally made up." Samantha said, cheerfully.

"Friends fight. Then they make up." Solene shrugged.

Friends. I tried to lock eyes with Samantha but she didn't look at me.

"Well I'm happy for you two…"

"Sam, what colleges have you applied to?" I interrupted before Solene could catch on.

"Probably every single one in the country." She laughed.

"Ara wants to go to Seattle for school." Solene said, nudging my knee from under the table.

"Seattle has been Ara's dream since she was a kid." Samantha smiled. It was true. Seattle was the city I fell in love with when my mother and father took me there. I was seven and I still remember looking up at the buildings in awe. The clam chowder we had at Ivar's. The ferry we took to Bainbridge. I told my mother I wanted to be here forever. She just shook her head and said the city corrupted young minds.

"Are you two going anywhere this summer, for a senior trip?" Samantha asked, taking a bite from her salad.

"My grandmother wants to go to Rome."

Solene never mentioned this before.

"Rome sounds…expensive." Samantha said. I gave her a dirty look. The rumors about her family's money were something Solene hated most. It took months before she confided in me about her inheritance. *My father was a lawyer and my mother a surgeon*, she explained.

"Ara is coming." Solene said, turning to me.

I didn't know how to respond with such a commitment

sprung on me. *Rome.*

"Yeah." I said, looking at Samantha who was now eyeing me as if to say *how will you afford that? How will your father ever allow that?* Samantha was always too reasonable. Too grown up.

"Sounds fun." Samantha finally said, though I knew she would interrogate me later for the details. I knew nothing. Solene could be making it up. Solene's feet tangled with mine and I had to hold back a smile. *Rome.* A place that existed only in my nightmares might become real. Tangible. Maybe the world will end once we're there, like some prophecy being fulfilled. Maybe this was our only chance to seal our fate. A fate that I know now would be tied together with tragedy.

After class that day Solene was waiting for me at the bike cage.

"You told Sam?" She said, calm and collected. I didn't know what to say. "I can tell by the way she watches us."

"I'm sorry." I sighed.

"It's fine." She shrugged.

"You're not mad?" I said, surprised.

"I don't want you telling everyone, but she's one of your best friends. I understand."

We were still navigating it all, fragile in our attempt to make sense of *this.*

"I won't tell anyone else. I swear."

"Ara." She murmured, looking around to see if there were any witnesses. The coast was clear. "I don't mean to be like this." Solene backed me against the brick wall, kissing me in a fervent way. "You're more than a secret." She spoke the words into my skin, as if it were meant to transfer to my bloodstream. I held her tight.

"We're going to Rome?" I asked.

"If you want to. My grandmother says she wants to see the colosseum before she dies and she's the one who mentioned inviting you."

"I don't have the money and my father would never let me..."

"Don't worry about the money and we just won't tell your father." She said, giving me a knowing look. *Let's run away.*

"He'll freak out."

"Just think about it. You even said it yourself this morning. You need to get away from this town. This is our chance." She kissed me once more before turning to retrieve her bike.

"A *temporary* fix." I said, grabbing my own bike.

"We'll figure out the rest as we go."

I knew I could trust her. I left it at that.

It was a warm winter day. Early in the morning, we went to the orange tree together. To me, it felt good to be this in love. I rolled onto her, tossing aside the copy of *Frankenstein* she was reading, and began to kiss her. She huffed into my mouth.

"Who's Phoebe?" Solene asked, abruptly. I froze against her lips, pulling away.

"Why?" I said, cautiously.

"Sam mentioned her."

"Sam should mind her own business."

"Just tell me who Phoebe is." Solene laughed.

"Remember the girl you rudely kicked out at Michael's party?"

"Oh." She paused. "I knew you slept with her that night. But I didn't know she

was the one who asked you out."

"We went on one date." I leaned in to resume the kiss, assuming there was nothing left to say. She put a hand to my lips and said, "Do you have feelings for her?"

"No, we're friends."

"Okay."

"Are you upset?" I said, studying her face, attempting to read her mind. She ran a hand through her hair, a habit she had whenever she was anxious.

"No, not at all." She said, now being the one to initiate a kiss. I didn't believe her.

"You coped by kissing boys, I coped by sleeping with a girl." I said, regretting it instantly as she yanked her arm from my grasp.

"Solene."

"Don't use that against me."

"You're the one who said you only liked boys. At Michael's party. You said that." I snapped, suddenly just as furious as she seemed to be. We fought for the rest of the night, from the orange tree all the way to my house and into my room. I cried like a child and she stormed out. Only to come back minutes later to kiss me with apologies and words that I never quite understood because we were both frantic. And that's how it went. We kissed, touched, made love, fought over stupid things, and lived a normal life. *I want a normal life with you*, I would tell her.

And that's how it went. A normal life.

Solene kept my troubles at bay, mostly troubles concerning my father. Since reuniting with Solene I was hardly ever home. Roaming the town with her, we'd get coffee and a pastry for breakfast; make our way to the museum, bookstores and the movies, ending the day in bed. Being in public had its challenges. I wanted to reach out and touch her just to see if she was *real*. I wanted to kiss her face anytime she made a funny joke. I wanted to say inappropriate thoughts every time they crossed my mind. But in the end, it was worth it. All that pent up lust resonated through my bones whenever we were alone. Here, beneath this orange tree, we were alone. Here, in my bedroom, *we were alone*. But we had to be careful at Solene's house, even if her bedroom door was locked. I respected her boundaries, suggesting we spend more time with her grandmother instead. That day, I sat at the kitchen table studying my history book. Vinos was now making dinner for us, Solene was talking to her in Arabic. I didn't mind being left out in conversations, I actually found their language to be comforting. Eventually Solene made her way back to the table, opening up her own book. We studied in silence until dinner was ready. Solene had expressed her fear of her grandmother finding out about us many times.

"You don't understand, Ara. My grandmother won't love me anymore."

"She'll never have to find out." I reassured her.

"She brought me to America when I was twelve because she believed I could have a better life. And this is how I repay her?" Solene cried in my arms. I bit my tongue. I couldn't judge her for how she chose her words, though hurtful. I understood.

My first acceptance letter came in the mail by springtime. It was for Antioch University in Seattle. I held the letter to my chest and breathed in. Hiding it before my father could see, I decided to tell no one. Solene didn't seem too worried that she hadn't received any letters yet. I was ready to chew through my fingernails, waiting to lose her. She had applied to colleges on the East Coast for a major in literature. How could I possibly exist on the West Coast without her? How could I possibly exist without her was the question that throbbed through me, ceaselessly and demonically. I needed her. And in return, I needed to be loved and accepted and desperately, *desperately* wanted. My obsession was not born of rationalization. This relationship resembled the first day of spring. Balmy and bright, the fresh earth cracked and probed by honey bees and amethyst. I was smelling wet sand and rising mist from the river, I couldn't comprehend a morning where she was not in my bed, lust dormant in our sheets from sleep. It stirs awake with the sun. But despite the delicacy of our love affair, my nightmares did not subside. Solene said I had a look of mourning in my sleep. I never told her about the dreams, even the ones where we fucked amid the apocalypse. Our need to find one another as the buildings were crumbling down and ash covered the sidewalks, was *desperate*. Our need to have one last orgasm together, even as hell opened up, was desperate. So when the time comes, maybe I will let her go to the East Coast and never look back. Maybe I will go to Seattle and forget her. Maybe my lies *will* catch up to me.

Solene used to live in Salt Lake City, Utah. Going to middle school in a conservative town was hard for her, but that's where she first met Stasia.

"Was Stasia your friend?"

"Stasia was the first girl I ever liked." Solene admitted.

"Did she know?" I asked. We were in my bedroom, I was braiding her hair, and the rain had started not too long ago.

"I think so."

"Did she feel the same way?"

"No." She said, turning to me once the braid was complete. Lying down on the bed, she looked up at the ceiling. "Stasia was the most popular girl in school, she had a handsome boyfriend. Things ended pretty badly between us."

"My first crush was in sixth grade. Her name was Melissa." I said, resting next to her.

"Did you hate yourself for it?"

"Yes." I paused, "I couldn't put a name to these feelings. When it came to Melissa, Charlotte, *you*..."

"Can you put a name to it now?" She whispered, turning onto her side to face me.

My heart was suddenly in my throat, we hadn't named what we had. Only in my head did I say it. *I love you.*

Instead of a verbal answer, I kissed her to let her know. I kissed her with all that I wanted to say. She held her eyes shut as she put her forehead to mine.

"احبّج." She said it with a kind of tenderness I did not know one could possess.

Although I didn't know her language, I somehow knew what she said. But still, I said nothing back in fear of being wrong.

My first encounter with death was when my childhood dog died. I watched from the driveway as a car ran them over, my mother and father running outside. My mother was crying, my father was shielding me from the gore. Maybe I was in shock, maybe I didn't know what death meant. But as we buried the dog in the backyard, I felt the heaviness. Placing the last drop of soil over the grave with my small hands. The house felt empty after that. No dog to greet me when I walked through the door, just an empty dog bed with its toys in the kitchen.

Rome was nearing. Life was manageable, and at times beautiful. As the end of our senior year neared, I was ready to let go of the idea that I would lose Solene. She was devoted to me more than ever. I was just as devoted. Perhaps we were delusional. Giving names to our unborn children, planning out the rest of our lives. How likely was it to have a happy life in secret? Solene said she might never be ready to come out, never be willing to hold my hand in front of others, never be willing to marry a girl. I wanted to tell her it gets easier, dealing with the shame. But I never did.

"I'll be the one looking for you, in every lifetime." I said, absorbing the smile in her eyes.

"I'll be waiting." Solene said, dancing her fingers up my arm. And just like that all my worries for our future would disappear.

"I have been *waiting* for you all my life, Solene." These moments were my favorite, the moments where we laid in my bed, naked, telling one another our deepest thoughts. Nothing could break us. I felt invincible. That's until she kissed me, like it was the last time.

"I was accepted to NYU. Full ride scholarship." She said, and my blood ran cold.

Chapter six

Harnessed to flesh

I bent like an orange tree in *her* wind. Endlessly forgiving all our flaws, I continued on as if nothing was different. But I knew, deep down, everything was coming to an end. Summer was nearing. This will be the last time for all of it. For all that we had. No more tasting her among the grass. We'll go to Rome, part ways. Then I'll go to Seattle and she'll go to New York.

"I'm so proud of you." I said, over and over again. She thanked me, kissing me with the strength of the sun. She'll never know how dark it got after that. I was now dreaming of *our* death vividly. Dying from the same sword, spilling faithful blood. The Mulberry tree, *our orange tree*. After I woke up in a pool of sweat, I saw my mother standing in the corner of the room. I didn't even have it in me to scream.

"I think I'm being haunted." I stated.

"Haunted by who?" Samantha said, not even looking up from her book. We were studying for finals at the local coffee shop. I had intentionally failed to invite Solene. I was selfishly avoiding her.

"My mother." I whispered.

"Ara." Samantha said, eyes widening as she placed her book on the table. I never spoke about my mother with her, so her surprise was warranted.

"And my father's anger is becoming worse." Before she

could answer, I continued on. "I don't want Solene to go to NYU."

"Have you told her that?" Samantha said, touching my hand for comfort.

"I can't. She's so happy. I can't ruin that for her." And that was that.

After a night at the movies, Solene asked if she could walk me home. I agreed. The night was beautiful, just as she was. My heart ached to see her now, the way she smiled so big. The moon was out and I kept my eye on it as we walked in silence. Would I lead a solitary life forever?

"Why are you so quiet?"

"You're quiet too." I replied.

"Are you okay?" She said, her walking had now ceased.

I wondered if she could feel the weight of my sorrow seeping from my pores.

"Kiss me." I said, as if it could fix everything.

She looked around, like she always did when we were in public. Then she was pulling me in by my waist, kissing me so delicately, I knew she was being careful in case I might break. I also knew we were pretending to not know what was really wrong with me.

"Better?" She said once the kiss ended.

"Yes."

We both weren't convinced.

"Stay with me tonight?"

"Of course." She smiled.

We stole some of my father's alcohol, wincing as

we drank it quickly. With each kiss, the whiskey began to taste nice in Solene's mouth. At times like this, I understood my father. I understood why he drank to drown out all the noise. I would never admit that to another person. I am my father's child.

"I'd still run away with you." I said, lacing our hands. We were drunk, tangled in sheets, and attempting to catch our breath. "Run away with me."

"Funny." Solene said, making her way down my body. I felt her tongue circling my nipple, I let out a soft gradual moan despite my anger. We continued on this way, her mouth doing all the work. We continued on even though I was seething. It was eating me alive. Before I knew it, I was breaking away from her.

"Why is that funny?"

"Oh, you were being serious."

"Is that so ridiculous to think?" I said, head pounding.

"Ara, I have NYU. I have responsibilities."

I studied her face, her ethereal face. *What about me? Is what I wanted to say. You're leaving me behind without a second thought.* I could have told her about Seattle. I could have said *I have my own future and my own responsibilities.*

"Yes, how could I possibly forget about NYU." I said, sarcastically. I knew this wasn't a good time to have this conversation, especially when I was completely wasted.

"Fuck you, Ara." Solene said. "I knew you couldn't be happy for me. You just want me all to yourself."

I didn't know whether to laugh or cry.

"Leave then." I didn't mean it.

"Ara..."

"Of course I'm happy for you." I began. But Solene was already all over me, holding me tightly.

"I'm sorry." She whispered.

"I think you hurt me more than you'll ever know." I whispered back.

"You hurt me too."

"Why are you with me?" I said, dejectedly.

"We could end this."

"You don't mean that." I was willing to beg.

"I don't. I'm just mad at you. We shouldn't say things until tomorrow."

I nodded, yielding to her completely. We resumed spreading each other's chest wide open. If this isn't love, then I want to know what it is.

The days were growing warmer. My fear of summer, *growing*, as though the pollen would close up my throat. The heat, a resemblance to her skin or maybe even hell, I was flying too close to the sun. *Forever Icarus.* I could feel doubt bubble up inside me. The hummingbirds were coming home to nest. Solene donated her bike and half her closet to the town's thrift shop. I felt wounded. A traitorous display of my emotions, I can't help but be human. As if contagious, we swapped scars every time we came in contact. I never complained. I will pull her into me each night, no matter the consequence.

"Long distance doesn't always work." I said after she hinted at it. It was a Thursday night. The humid night air was coming through the window.

"What are you saying?"

"I'm not saying anything..."

"Long distance isn't an option for you?"

"I didn't say that." I snapped. Solene rolled her eyes and stood up from my bed.

"Why don't we just throw in the towel." She said, aggressively dressing herself.

"Come back to bed."

"No."

"Fine." I sat up with the sheet still wrapped around me. "Long distance isn't ideal but I feel like it could work." The need to beg was crawling back up my throat.

"Are you just saying that or do you really mean it?"

I hesitated and she was already out of the room. I laid back down. I didn't have it in me to chase her. These days all we did was fight. One of us is always storming away. I texted *sorry* to her, but when there was no reply I went to bed with a knot in my stomach. Did she really want to end this? *Solene, if you do, make it quick. Make it a mercy killing.*

I had a savior complex. My mother was the first one I thought I could save. If I prayed, if I wore a cross, and if I kept a picture of Jesus by my bedside; then maybe she would love me enough to stay. My father was next. I got used to the smell of whiskey, I made sure to roll him on his side after he passed out. I even diluted his bottles of alcohol with water so he wouldn't get so mean. If I kept the house clean, if I cooked for him, and if I left him alone by tiptoeing around; then maybe he'd go back to loving me like a father should. Solene was someone I could never save. I failed in the end. If I gave her pleasure, if I worshiped her, and if I buried myself within her; then maybe she would do the same. But they all took something from me that I'll never get back. I'll never get back what I lost each time my world came to an end.

"Ara." I heard someone whisper. "Ara, wake up."

"What." I groaned. I opened my eyes, rolling out of bed and realized the voice was coming from outside my open window. I stood on my toes to get a better look, only to see Solene standing there.

"What are you doing?" I hissed. It was seven in the morning.

"Just let me in." She said, already rounding the corner of the house to meet me at the front door. I snuck her in, closing the door quietly as she went straight to my room without a word.

"Ara..."

"I know what you're going to say." I said, knees ready to buckle.

"Then let me say it." Solene snapped.

"Fine." I crossed my arms.

"I'm leaving for NYU in a couple weeks."

I knew she was here to end *this*. Whatever *this* was. She had mentioned our fate so often over the past couple days, it was ingrained into me.

"I want you to come with me." She said, unexpectedly.

"You want me to come to New York with you?"

"Yes."

"You don't want to break up?"

"No." She frowned. "Why would you think that?"

I shrugged. She approached me with a kiss, pushing the hair from my shoulders. I felt relief and, all at once, I felt *her*. Inside me, around me, between each rib. I was stripped down to the very bone for her. And all at once, I remembered Seattle. I chose to say nothing. My acceptance letter was hiding in a drawer behind her. I chose to ignore it.

Limestone turned to dust as we rested in the amphitheater, hiding away while the rest of the world caught fire. Naked, bathing in the sun that is now a red giant, I felt the ground tremble. We ignored the sirens that blared throughout the city, warning us to run and take cover. *But we were occupied.*

"I think the world is ending." Solene said, biting my lip.

"The world *is* ending." I said, licking off ash that had settled on her skin. I had this ungodly feeling, this sinking feeling. We were being torn from each other.

"Ara."

"Solene, don't leave me."

"Ara!"

I felt something tugging on me, rocking me back and forth. My eyes fluttered open, Solene was laying next to me as she held on tight to my shoulder.

"Are you okay?" Solene said, "I've been trying to wake you up but you just kept crying and saying my name."

"Yeah, just a bad dream."

"Do you want to talk about it?"

"No." I said, "Just go back to bed."

I couldn't fall asleep after that, just holding her in my arms, feeling her hot breath on my neck. Graduation had passed and so had our final exams, nothing was left but to pack my things for Rome. I had my reservations, ones Samantha brought up. *Where are you going to live? What are you going to do? Just not go to school and follow her across the country? With what money? What does your father say?*

Every story had its end. I had Solene. I was going to New York to be with her. I was getting out of this town, away from my father's contempt. So why did I feel this way? So disconnected from it all, I was ready to admit to myself that this wasn't the life I envisioned. I thought when I grew up, I would be so much more than this. My younger self would mourn for me. Would she hate me like I do?

It was one hundred degrees today, the air thick with hesitancy, I was fanning myself when suddenly Solene was climbing on top of me.

"Are you excited?"

"What am I going to do in New york?"

"Be with me." Solene said. I knew she was joking but it didn't help.

"Yes, but Sam thinks..."

"Are you second guessing this?" She frowned. I pulled her into me and sighed.

"I'm just... I don't know."

Solene got up from where we were lying on the grass under the orange tree. I tried to take her hand but she yanked it away.

"I have to go." Solene said. I knew she didn't. Curfew wasn't for another hour.

Later that night, I was in bed reading when I heard the front door slam shut with a bang. I jumped up in a hurry. In the living room stood my father, leaning against the wall.

"What's wrong?" I said, keeping my distance.

"Ara, go away." He said through gritted teeth.

I wasn't ready to deal with him today and his moods, so I turned away to lock myself in my room. That's when I heard my father collapse onto the couch, his weeping hard to ignore.

"I'm sorry kiddo, I'm so sorry." He cried and cried, reaching for me. I gravitated to his pain. I too wanted to cry at that moment, but I knew it wouldn't make things better. I learned to talk less when I was around him. Hours passed and he was now fast asleep, I could still smell the liquor as I walked to my room. I picked up my phone, eager to see if Solene had messaged me. But nothing. There was a black hole in my chest that absorbed everything good in my life. I wanted to *want* New York so badly. *Don't hate me. I'm still trying to learn how to be happy. I still want to run away with you. We can teach each other how to be happy.* Every word I typed out seemed like it would be the end of us if I hit send. I couldn't lose her. *I'm a coward. I will follow you anywhere.* I sent it, holding my breath. She replied almost immediately. *I adore you, Ara. More than anything.*

By the time I went to tell my father where I was going, it was far too late. He had found out from my journal, which was now in his hands when I walked into my room after a day with Solene.

"You're going to college. You're not leaving for New York…"

"I'm eighteen in August, I can leave whenever I want." It was now a full on screaming match, his anger growing with each word I spoke.

"I'm not going to let you throw away your life over a girl you think you're in love with."

"I'm almost eighteen!" That was the only argument I could convene.

"You're still a child!"

"I'm not a child." I said. "Why the fuck are you going through my journal anyways?"

"Don't you dare talk to me like that, Ara." He spat. "I'm still your father."

"Hardly." I said, recoiling as he threw my journal across the room. He stepped toward me and I thought *he's going to hit me.* I hid my face like a scared little kid and felt a whimper escape from me. Then he was gone. I collapsed onto the floor, shaking uncontrollably. After I regained some feeling back in my limbs, I stood and began to pack the few items that held meaning to me. I waited until dark to leave, heading straight to Solene's house. I knew she'd still be awake, it was only nine p.m. Vinos was the one who opened the door as I stood there with my backpack, mascara running down my cheeks. Her eyes widened, but with complete sincerity. I put my arms around her and she held on tight, murmuring

"زين كلشي راح يصير."

I saw Solene walk out into the front room from over Vinos' shoulder.

"Ara, what's wrong?" Solene asked. Vinos let me go and turned to Solene.

"Can I stay here tonight?" I said. Solene spoke Arabic to Vinos and Vinos nodded. I felt safe.

"Are you going to tell me what happened?" Solene said once we were in her room.

"My dad found out about New York and *us*."

The color drained from my Solene's face.

"He didn't even care about you and I being together." I laughed bitterly. "But I thought he was going to hit me after I implied he wasn't a good father."

"If he laid a hand on you... I'll kill him." Solene said.

"I can't go back to that house. I can't spend one more second there." I whispered.

"Listen, we'll be in Rome soon and he won't be able to find you."

"But he'll find us in New York."

"You'll be eighteen by then. He won't have any say in

your life anymore. It will all work out, Ara." Solene took me into her arms as I shut my eyes. I lived in this purgatory between hoping things will change and knowing that they won't.

"You can stay here until we leave for Rome." Solene said, kissing every part of my face until I folded.

I went home the next day when I knew my dad would be at work. I grabbed a couple more items and my passport, attempting to leave my room in order rather than to hint at my plan to run away. I wrote out a note and left it on the kitchen counter.

I'm staying at Solene's for the week.

That way he wouldn't be worried until it was too late. I'll be halfway to Rome. I didn't know why I felt like mourning. I wanted out of this town for so long and now it was actually happening, I had this sudden thought of missing all that I had. I'll miss the orange tree. I'll miss writing at the local cafe. I'll miss reading on the dock. I'll miss riding my bike up the canyon. *I'll miss my father.* It was wishful thinking and a symptom of romanticizing a life that was no good. I walked out of my house and took one look before leaving. I took one look and I nearly ran back inside. But *inside* there will be no mother to hug. No dog to greet me. No father to make proud. I walked back to Solene's, feet trailing on the ground as their weight held me down. Solene was standing on her front porch, waiting.

"Hey." I muttered, dropping my bag. My arms were tired and I was sweating.

"Hey." She said, stepping closer.

"I left a note."

"Are you okay?"

"I don't think so." I was wiping away a tear before I realized there were too many to catch.

"Your father can't hurt you anymore."

"Is it wrong that I'll miss him?"

Solene made a face that I took as judgment. "Ara, think of everything he's done to you."

"Doesn't mean I hate him."

"Well I hate him." Solene said, angrily.

"Please, *don't*."

"I'll try. For you."

I didn't have it in me to tell her I was wanting to go back. To leave her. I had this feeling I should run. Go to Seattle and never look back. And then I felt sick. How could I ever leave her? She's all I had left.

"Let's get you inside." Solene said, picking up my bags. I followed her. The kind of evil that my mother spoke of trailed in behind.

I showered that night, stepping out of the tub to look in the mirror. The steam distorted my image into something demonic so I wiped the mirror in a hurry. My hair was dripping water onto the floor but I just continued to stare at myself. I did look like my mother. But I had my father's nose. I didn't really know who I was. Who I belonged to.

Pieced together by all those who have destroyed me, I was left with dysphoria.

"Dinner is ready." Solene said from the other side of the door.

"Coming." I said, snapping out of my trance. I took one more look at my mouth and smiled. I smiled big, with teeth. It looked like I was in pain. I smiled and it looked like I was the first human ever who just learned how to smile.

"Is your grandmother really okay with me staying here all week?"

"I said your dad was out of town." Solene whispered. It was late. I was feeling a little better, full with a homemade meal and resting in her arms. She was being as affectionate as ever.

"What was your father like?" I asked.

"He was a very stern man. But with me, his edges softened. He liked to make jokes and see me laugh."

"My father used to be the same way." I paused, "Before my mother..."

"I'm sorry about earlier. I just can't stand knowing the way he treats you."

"Sometimes I'm afraid it's my own fault."

"What do you mean?"

"What if I'm not a good daughter?" I said, shifting away because of the sudden emotion that came over me. "What if I've never been good?"

"You're good, Ara. You're more than good." She insisted, pulling me in as I remained limp. *Am I good for you,*

Am I good for you? As good as a martyr.

The week passed by quickly. Still no word from my father. I figured he had nothing to say after reading my note. But on the day we left for Rome, my father called seven times in the same hour. I ignored every single one, scared he'd come looking for me. On the way to the airport, I gripped Solene's hand in the backseat while her grandmother sat in the front seat of the Uber. She squeezed my hand in a way that should've hurt. I loved her and I couldn't help but love her. Could I ever stop? I was starting to believe it was impossible not to.

When I think back to that night at the airport, I remember my knee jumping in place and Solene whispering to her grandmother in Arabic. I was paralyzed. Solene would say things to me but I would not respond.

Your father is looking for you and said you won't answer his calls.

The text came from Samantha as we were boarding the plane.

Don't tell him about Rome. Please, Sam.

I turned off my phone and closed my eyes. I felt Solene nudge me to go forward.

"Ma'am I need to scan your ticket." The woman said. I turned to Solene with all that I could not say flooding my eyes. She nodded and gave the lady my ticket herself. Solene then led me to our seats, waving goodbye to Vinos who was sitting a couple rows down from us.

"Are you okay?" Solene said in a hushed tone.

"Are we making a mistake?"

"Nothing with you is a mistake." Solene said.

"What's the plan again?" I felt nauseous.

"We'll spend however long we need to in Rome..."

"We only booked the trip for six days..."

"We'll handle that when the time comes."

"Okay."

"We have to stay away from the States until your father realizes you're not coming back."

I nodded. I was leaving behind everything I had ever known. Looking back on that night, I saw myself as the villain of my own story. My father, Samantha, the grave of my mother; all left in the wake of my own selfish destruction. Didion's words rang through my head, *What makes Iago evil? Some people ask. I never ask.*

part two

"She was a gentle sort of horror."

— Julia Armfield

Chapter seven

We are all just trying to be holy

Fourteen hours later and Rome appeared. When we were off the plane and exiting the airport I became painfully aware of my body and the absence of my father. However abusive or perhaps just sick, I still loved him. I still craved that parental affection. But did I want it just as much as I wanted Solene? I wasn't sure. I have felt doubt even when it came to her.

"Check-in time is soon." Solene said, waving down a taxi and then turning to me with a smile. I felt a little better knowing she was content. I turned on my phone, only to find fifteen missed calls from Samantha and thirty from my father. My stomach sank. The cops had probably already tracked my location. They'll be here any minute to put an end to this.

"Solene." I whispered. "My phone." I showed her all the missed calls and texts that I couldn't bring myself to read. She took the phone from me in a hurry and stuffed it in her pocket.

"I'll take care of it." She murmured. I trusted her.

The ride in the taxi was long and awkward. Solene and her grandmother argued for most of it, voices raising, while I watched the taxi driver's eyes dart to the road and then to the rearview mirror. I pressed my face to the cool glass of the car window and pretended I didn't just fly thousands of miles just for me to feel the same as I always did. By the time we arrived at the hotel, I was ready to sleep. The driver helped unload our bags as a bellhop came outside to load everything onto a cart that looked like it was made of real gold.

Vinos was staying in her own suite, while Solene and I were sharing a room that had two queen beds. The rooms had high ceilings, with smooth pale hardwood floors and giant brown curtains that covered the windows. I thanked Vinos and she gave me a tight hug and a kiss on the cheek. Solene said her goodnight, shutting the door and locking it gently so no one on the other side could have their suspicions.

"We'll have to undo both beds each night so it looks like we slept separately." Solene said, walking into the bathroom with her luggage. I went to lay on the bed closest to the window, hearing her brush her teeth and then shower. *Slept separately.* I brushed the thought away, now curious to know what my new life had in store for me. I was slowly opening up to the idea of having my own free will, with Solene by my side, and writing poetry on the balcony of whichever hotel we chose to stay at that week. Vagabonds. Bandits. I was suddenly buzzing with exhilaration. Solene finally emerged from the bathroom, wet hair tangled around her bare shoulders. I smiled, knowing she chose to walk back into this room naked *just for me*.

"No one can find us here?"

"No one can find us here." Solene said, kneeling on the bed. I placed a hand on her cheek and she kissed the side of my palm.

"We'll be together, always?"

"Always." She said, now crawling into my space to give me a kiss of reassurance. I kissed her back, fervently. With her tongue in my mouth, I nearly said it, I nearly said it all. *I love you. I'd die for you. I'd die over and over again just to be a part of you. Let me be a part of you like the seeds are for the oranges. I love you, you're the love of my life.*

She removed my clothes with fluidity, moaning as I placed a hand between her legs. I told her to be quiet, covering her mouth. She looked at me, her brown eyes conveying all that I felt. We were cocooned by the erotic sensation that surged between us.

"Please, don't stop." Solene said, moving her hips to the rhythm of my hand.

I could never stop. Like a carnivorous sundew, I was trapped in her nectar. After she finished, she went down between my thighs and pressed her mouth to my pubic bone. I shuddered. She teased me for a while, probably seeing if she could get me to beg. I was stubborn. I eventually climaxed, with my hands in her hair.

"Was I too loud?" I asked.

"You were perfect." She said, drawing me into her arms. I now wasn't afraid of Rome or being away from California. I was *afraid* of losing her. A deep rooted fear that lived in me, right beside my lungs. When I would breathe, I was reminded just how great that loss really could be.

Whenever Charlotte came over to play house, I'd tell

her she was my wife. We'd handled our fake baby with care, patting her on the back as Charlotte sang her to sleep. We ate pretend meals together and even hugged as I left for my pretend job. It wasn't until later on, did I feel shame for wanting that reality. For wanting a real wife to come home to. Being friends with girls never felt normal to me. That's why I cried in my mother's arms when Charlotte moved away and that's why I cried when Melissa turned the whole school against me after I tried to kiss her inside that gymnasium. Graceless, without any sense, I wandered through life wondering what was wrong with me. How could every boy I kiss repel me? Wanting to disprove my hypothesis, I decided sex with a boy was the only solution. Oliver was cute, popular; I asked him if I could come over while his parents were out of town. We watched two movies before he made a move, already hard as he pressed into me. I felt lifeless. I went home and cried, wishing I could cry in my mother's arms, but she had been gone for six years now. I continued to sleep with random men, some older than me, some my age. Each time felt worse, a downward spiral that I had no intention of stopping. Some of them wouldn't stop when I asked, some even guilted me into it because *I had already turned them on and it wasn't fair if we stopped now.* I gave up after Eric. He said I wasn't his type anyways and he kicked me out of his car. The following week the new girl appeared in town.

"How did you sleep?" I asked, chin resting on her

chest. The curtains were wide open, revealing Rome to us like a fruit we were ready to bite into.

"I slept good. And you?"

"I've never slept so good." I said, truthfully. No nightmares, no apocalypse. Just absolute peace in our little hotel room. The white comforter was wrapped around us, giant and fluffy.

"Room service?" She said, reaching for the phone on the bedside table.

"Room service sounds great." I said, squeezing her hand.

When there was a knock at the door, Solene put on a robe and looked through the peephole to make sure it was a hotel worker and not her grandmother. She gave me a thumbs up and cracked the door open, thanking them as they handed her a silver tray. She brought it to the bed, plopping a grape into her mouth. After we stayed up most of the night, taking advantage of the alone time, I was now starving. The platter was filled with various fruits, french toast, eggs and bacon. I turned on the television, changing the channel until I found something familiar. Turning my attention back to the food, I poured syrup over the french toast and offered some to Solene. She took the fork into her mouth and chewed thoughtfully. I loved this. I loved the simplicity. *Arsenic and Old Lace* continued on in the background as we fed each other, kissing between each bite.

"What should we do today?" Solene said, tucking my hair behind my ear.

"I'm not sure. I don't know much about Rome."

"Come on, let's get dressed. I'll take you for some coffee."

Solene checked on Vinos, who was still feeling tired and a bit under the weather. She said Vinos wanted us to still go out and enjoy our time. After that we went down to the front desk. They gave us several tourist pamphlets, recommending a coffee shop down the street that also happened to have a bicycle shop next to it. We had a plan to bike around the city, just as we did in our small town, except this time we'd have to find another tree to lounge beneath. Walking down the cobbled street, I felt our hands brush. Solene was wearing a dress, sleeves slipping over her tanned shoulders, hazel hair bright against the white fabric.

"There's no one in this city who knows us." I said, "They wouldn't even bat an eye if I kissed you right here."

Solene stopped in her tracks.

"That's not funny, Ara."

"I'm not trying to be funny."

"We can't. You know I can't." She whispered. Even in a foreign country, our love was seen as impermissible to her.

At the cafe we ordered two lattes and sat outside on the small tables that lined the building. I sipped on my mug, looking around. Solene was looking at me.

"What?" I said.

"Are you mad at me?"

"No."

"Because if you were, I'd understand."

"Well, I'm not."

We were the only ones out here, surrounded by ivy and brick, so I guess that's why she felt safe enough to reach across the table and take my hand.

"There. Better?" She said, softly. When the bell of the cafe door rang, she dropped my hand instantly. I looked away from her. Later, after renting two bikes, we rode past a fruit stand. Solene pulled out her plastic bag of euros and asked for two oranges. We continued on, speeding down every narrow street, past the rustic villages, over the Ponte Sisto that hung above the Tiber river, and to Trilussa square. Placing our bikes on the ground, we rested on the stone steps, looking up to the clear blue sky. Not one cloud littered above. Solene handed me an orange from her backpack. I peeled mine with careful consideration.

"I love being with you." I said, feeling the heat of the sun bathe me. There were others, groups of teenagers and parents crowding the steps, having picnics, laughing and speaking in what I guessed to be Italian.

"You love it even if I'm a coward?" Solene said, putting a slice of orange into her mouth. I was brought back to the night we first slept together. How the juices transpired between us, how I could still taste *her*, how we were in our own inhabitable world.

"I don't think you're a coward." I said, truthfully. Solene edged closer to me so our bony knees were now touching. It was a start.

"We'll have our own place in New york. We'll get a

dog. We'll even have our own coffee maker so I can make it for you every morning." Solene whispered. I felt my insides ache. The good kind of *ache*. An ache that conquered all other aches true blue to grief.

"What will we name our dog?" I wanted her to go on and on. I wanted to hear more about the life she imagined for us.

"We'll name her Sappho. Saph for short."

I laughed and rolled my eyes.

"Too on the nose?"

"Yeah, a bit." I said, finishing my orange. "Solene, if you want a life of secrecy then I'm willing to hide away for the rest of my life."

We sat in silence. People watching and skimming through the books we brought with us. Mine, Lousie Gluck's poetry collection. Solene's was Deathless by Catherynne M. Valente. She leaned into me and pointed to a line she had highlighted. *A machine for loving you. Nothing in me was not made by you.* I wanted to kiss her right there, in Trilussa square, for everyone to see. I wanted her to make love with me against the ancient monuments so the voices of Rome would know just how much *we* wanted it.

I almost reached over to have her taste my spoon of gelato but I stuffed the spoon into my own mouth and felt embarrassed. Solene didn't seem to notice.

"What if you get tired of hiding away?" Solene said, studying her spoon before licking it.

"I won't get tired. Not when it's with you."

"I get tired of myself." Solene murmured. She didn't mention her self doubt to me much, but neither did I. I was terrible for the way I perceived myself. As something demented, unappetizing and pessimistic.

"Just finish your gelato." I said, smiling. She smiled back, nudging my foot from under the table. We were in an ice cream shop, watching the waves of tourists pour in and out during the evening time. The pinkish glow from the window highlighted her hazel hair iridescently. It brought me back to the schoolyard, where I first saw her. *The new girl.* My lungs desiccated at the sight of her.

"What took you so long?" I said, leaning forward after my gelato was finished. Solene raised her brow in confusion, so I gave more clarity. "You should have kissed me that night, in that hallway, at Michael's party when we first met. What took you so long?"

"Ara..."

"I knew you felt it."

"I did, I did." She whispered, nearly breathless. I knew no one could hear us. The Italian opera was loud on the speakers above, along with the customers surrounding us. But still, Solene said, "Not here."

We left the shop and walked until there wasn't another person in sight. Finally, Solene turned to me, biting her lip. A thing she did when she was nervous.

"I know. I wasted time. I wasted your time. So many times I could have kissed you. But I will make it up to you. I swear I will." Solene said, taking my hand.

I knew I wasted just as much; I wasted away, I wasted myself as a person. I'm still finding ways to be forgiving. Forgiveness in my dreamland was built from scar tissue. *Solene, I bleed when I attempt to let anyone in. It strips me naked when I trust someone. But for you, I will become unlocked.*

"Come here." I said, pulling her in gently.

"I was so afraid. What if I got it wrong? What if I misread your signals?" She said against my mouth. I kissed her once before stepping back. The warmth was dropping in the air. I shivered as she rubbed the sides of my arms. We could stand here for hours and try to dissect every interaction we ever had as friends, and try to understand how we missed it. How we missed the feelings we harbored for one another. *How we longed to melt our bodies together and together and together, until our bones were one.*

"I have you now." I said. *I have you now. No one could ever love you as I have loved you.*

"You have me." She said, nodding with our foreheads together. Our eyes met and I could tell her thoughts in an instant grew impure. Impure in the way that meant *I want to devour you.* I kissed her softly and she pushed her tongue into my mouth. This kiss was a work of art. I could feel it in real time, the way the artist could convey our devotion and hunger. The brushstrokes, pretty and abstract.

"I have an idea." Solene said, excitedly. She kissed me and then she was telling me to wait here. *I'll be right back.*

I had seldomly thought back to the signs that we were

something awful. But then again, I never thought about our missteps. I thought about *this*, this night where we were in the city, drinking alcohol in an alleyway that Solene had just bought. I was now hunched over, dry heaving. Solene held my hair the entire time.

"Let's go back to the hotel." She said, rubbing my back. I could hear nearby street music, I could feel the remaining liquor swimming in my head. The fresh night air felt sobering. I inhaled deeply and pushed out a breath that assured me I was okay enough to ride my bike. Solene and I rode out of the alleyway, introduced to a nightlife that was high spirited and enchanting, the streets fringed with a string of lights.

"Wooohooo!" Solene shouted, letting go of the handle bars as we zoomed past a group of girls dancing. I felt wide awake. I felt homesick. I felt alive. I felt alone. I stretched out my arms along with her and held open my mouth to mime a scream. *I had seldomly thought back to the signs that we were something awful.* I almost hit the brakes to regain my composure. I could feel my eyes burning. My stomach *in* knots. I was coming undone. Solene was carefree and far ahead of me. All the men whistled as she rode past. I wanted nothing to do with her. I wanted to follow her until my feet bled from pedaling.

"Ara, catch up!" Solene said from over her shoulder. And I did.

My father taught me how to ride a bike at six years old, as my mother watched nervously from the yard. I fell the first time, scraping my knee, and my mother flocked over to me, pushing my father aside.

"I told you she wasn't ready." She hissed, placing the fabric of her dress over the flowing wound.

"I can do it." I said, determined.

"See." My father said, using his hand to ruffle my hair.

It took only a couple more tries before I was down the block, without the help of my father's hands to balance me. By the time I circled the neighborhood and made my way back home, my mother and father were nowhere to be seen. I was hoping I'd at least see my father's smile as he clapped in amazement. Once inside I heard the familiar cries that escaped from my mother and the gentle hushes from my father. I sat outside their bedroom and listened to her cry until it was dark, the only light was from her dim bedside lamp. I didn't understand the weight of her sadness. I didn't understand how one moment she was on her feet, smiling, a half functioning human, and the next she was staring at the wall. I didn't understand at six, nor at seven, not even at eight. But it eventually clicked. I will *never* forget when it clicked.

It was midnight by the time we reached the hotel. Solene, still drunk, couldn't get the door open to our room. I took the key card from her hand, lingering my fingers on her wrist. She turned to me with a kind of yearning I could not ignore. I pressed her into the door, kissing her slowly as if it were a question. She responded by taking my hand and placing it on her breast.

"We shouldn't do this in the hallway." She said, sliding her hand underneath my skirt. I heard someone's door nearby begin to open. We broke apart. *We really shouldn't be doing this in the hallway.* I slid the key card into the slot and heard the beep of admission. Safely inside, we began to tear into each other, bloodthirsty and titillated. I felt my entire body hum with satisfaction, Solene's hand unrelentingly inflicting so much pleasure. I couldn't help but chant her name until I climaxed.

"Thank you." I sighed into her shoulder, my leg hitched around her waist. She was still using all her strength to hold me up against the wall. "Thank you." I repeated it like a prayer until it had no meaning. We killed all that got in our way so we could be alone. Now we were left with a corpse to dispose of.

My dreams were apparently still a space for constant wretchedness. That night, as my eyes slowly drifted shut, I saw a blinding light. The sun was up in red flames, close enough to the earth to melt the skin off bones. And there was Solene, standing by the rising sea on a cliffside. I went to say her name, to warn her not to drown. But nothing escaped my mouth. Only a mouth full of blood. She jumped and the waves swallowed her whole. I woke up choking on nothing, sitting up in a panic. It was morning time and Solene's side of the bed was empty. I heard shouting in the next room over and then a door slam belligerently. Solene walked back into our room seconds later, completely exerted.

"What happened?" I asked. I had felt the tension between her and Vinos in the taxi. Something was clearly wrong.

"My grandma found out your father didn't know we were coming here."

"What? How? Is she going to make me go back?"

"It's okay." Solene said, sitting on the bed to touch my hand. "She's mad, but I explained to her that your father is an alcoholic."

"I'm sorry, this is all my fault." I said, looking down.

"Ara, everything is fine." She said, kissing me before springing up off the bed. "Vinos wants to see the Colosseum today. Get ready."

I remember my mother wanted to baptize me. My father said no. They fought over my innocence like a chew toy. I went into my mother's closet that day and found a white button down shirt to try on. The sleeves flowed past my hands, the hem to my knees. I climbed in the bathtub of warm water and laid there until it turned cold. I didn't feel any different. I dipped my head under the water and held my breath as I counted to ten. My mother walked into the bathroom and pulled me out, scolding me for ruining her clothes. I wanted her to love me. I wanted her to see me as *holy*. I fought tooth and nail for that very holiness until it ingested me and spat me back out. I now *believe* Solene made me holy, I believed it until the very end.

124

Chapter eight

Spit the blood back

I never imagined loving someone in the way I loved Solene. And even after all these years, everyone will still know her name because I carry it with me. I created a shrine out of all the parts of me she touched. I was a walking sacrifice for her altar.

I sit here sipping on her leftover coffee. Vinos was waiting for us down in the lobby, but Solene couldn't find her favorite pair of jeans. The high waisted ones that flared at the bottom and had a small hole by the second belt loop.

"Wear these." I said, handing her a pair of mine. They fit her perfectly. I felt *something* seeing her wear my clothes, I felt deeply.

"Thanks." She smiled. I studied her, the way she walked across the room, letting her hair down as she put on a fitted crop top. Her natural beauty, so prominent. I never was jealous when others had to stop to look at her. How could I compare? With my rudimentary eyes, dull hair, and pale skin, I was nowhere near the standards she deserved. But when Solene looked at me and said my eyes were as blue as Dijlah, I believed her. She said my skin was like porcelain, my hair luscious and dripping honey, my body like a hellenistic sculpture. I *believed* every word.

"Has Sam texted you?"

"Yes." Solene said, phone in hand and backpack on

one shoulder.

"What did she say?"

"She's worried. I told her not to be."

"Can I call her?"

"If you think that's a good idea." Solene said, "You can call on the way to the Colosseum." Before we went out the door, I cupped her face and gave her a kiss. She kissed me back. We both knew this room would be waiting for us by the end of the day. That's what made it all worth it.

Once in the cab, Solene handed me her phone and with shaky hands I scrolled to Samantha's name. I hesitantly hit the call button and wondered if she would pick up with the time difference. On the fourth ring I heard *hello*.

"Sam, it's me." I said, tearing up at her familiar voice.

"Ara, your dad is going crazy."

"You can't tell him where I am."

"He's your father..."

"He's an alcoholic who almost hit me."

"I won't tell." Samantha sighed. "Are you okay? How's Rome?"

"I'm more than okay." My head had never been clearer. "Listen, I don't think I'm coming back."

"What do you mean you're not coming back?"

"I've said too much..."

"Ara, you can trust me."

"I have to go."

After I hung up, I wiped away my quiet tears. Solene squoze my hand. Samantha had been there for me since I was eleven, now she was across the world. Would I ever see her again? I didn't even know what my life would look like a week from now. How could I be so sure I'd ever cross paths with my past again?

"Why is your father always so angry?"

"I'm sorry."

"Don't apologize." Samantha whispered. We were hiding in my closet, hearing the breaking of dishes. My father was drunk and couldn't find another bottle of whiskey. He usually trashed the kitchen until he eventually just left for the bar. I don't think he knew I was home. His anger could be felt through the wall. I knew Samantha was terrified. Her *home* was safe, clean, with parents who never even raised their voices. I was fourteen years old at this point, too old to be playing hide and seek.

"If you want to, you can move in with me."

"You should go home, Sam. Sneak out the window." I said, immune to the hope of finding a safe place for myself.

"Will you be okay?"

I smiled, halfheartedly. A lukewarm response to a question I had not been able to answer truthfully in my life. Samantha hugged me goodbye and was out the window before my father heard a sound. I thought from that day forward Samantha would never come to my house again but she was loyal. My chosen family. She kept me safe until I was no longer afraid. I just eventually grew numb to it. I grew numb to all that stripped me like raw meat.

127

This is where I dreamt the world was ending is what I wanted to say when we stepped out into the box overlooking the arena. Everyone around us spoke of gladiators, fights to the death, naval battles; I looked to the collapsed parts of the amphitheater that had been inflicted by natural disasters. I thought of the earth trembling. I thought of the stone crumbling around Solene and I. Spectators would watch in horror. I would be *watching* Solene. They'll see us getting undressed on top of the rubble. They wouldn't understand. It didn't matter. This was our last chance.

"What do you think?" Solene asked, leaning over the terrace to get a better look. "I've never seen anything like it." I said, shielding my face from the sun as I snapped out of my existential daydream. Vinos looked at me with a smile that didn't reach her eyes. I can't feel it, nor know *it* yet, but the color that drained from her face should've been the first sign.

We stopped for pizza and spritz after we left the colosseum. Solene and Vinos were busy talking so my lack of conversation went unnoticed. I felt inclined to ask if we could go back to the hotel but I didn't want to ruin the evening. We were, after all, having a nice day. Vinos motioned for the check and stared at me, now murmuring something to Solene.

"She wants to know what's wrong with you?"

"Nothing's wrong with me." I said, sincerely. *I* couldn't even put a name to this feeling that I had. Solene turned to her grandmother talking quickly, and then Vinos was laughing. The sky was pitch black by the time we arrived at the hotel.

"Ara..." Solene began, once we entered our room.

"I need a shower." I said, stripping off my clothes as if they were weighing me down.

"Did I do something wrong?" Solene said, following me into the bathroom. I leaned down to turn the faucet on.

I wanted to be cruel and say *not everything is about you* but it was, it truly was. And after all, she *was* the reason I dreamt of calamity. Wasn't she?

"Solene, there's a lot we don't tell each other." I said, stepping in, relaxing immediately as the hot water hit my shoulders. I was hoping she'd just leave after that but instead she opened the glass door, already undressed, and walked in. "What do you want to know?" She said. I watched the water trickle down over her breasts.

"You don't want to tell me. And I know you're traumatized. So why would I make you talk about it?"

"I'll talk about Iraq. Whatever you want..."

"It's just not that, Solene. Do you even know about *my* religious trauma?"

"How could I know if you don't tell me about it?" She asked.

"Maybe I don't know what I'm trying to say, but... the nightmares haven't stopped since the day I met you." I admitted, angrily. The atmosphere grew vampiric.

"I ask about your dreams almost every morning and I

129

get nothing from you." Solene snapped.

"What if the only way of getting to know each other is through sex?" I said after a long pause.

"Is that really such a bad thing?" She murmured, lashes dripping as she stepped closer.

I was ready to give in, anger evaporating. I kissed her under the stream of water, feeling my back hit the cold tile of the wall as she kissed me back. We were as urgent as a hurricane, crashing into each other like waves stirred up by Poseidon.

When she kissed me like this, it was like I could read her mind. I saw her walk into a lush green yard, pushing open the gate only to find a trail of bodies leading to the neighbor's date tree. A blood curdling scream. And then I was pushing her away, shaking my head frantically.

"Ara, what's wrong?" Solene said, pinning my hands down to my side as I began to cry.

"I don't know." I whispered. The water had now turned cold. Solene shut the shower off, wrapping a towel around me as she walked me to the bed.

"I know you." Solene said, sitting across from me. "I know you, Ara Lee Clemens. I know your favorite color is a pale yellow, not too bright. Your childhood dog's name was Willow. Your lucky number is five, which is so random. Your favorite poet is a tie between Plath and Audre Lorde. You have a small scar on the back of your knee..."

"How did I get the scar?"

"A rollerskating accident when you were seven." Solene

smiled, shyly. And then it faded. "I know how your mother died, but you've never gone into detail about it. I just figured I'd give you more time to open up..."

"I don't mean to hold back from you." I said, taking her hand.

"I don't mean to, either." She said, scooting closer as our foreheads pressed together. I closed my eyes, afraid to see more death. Because that's a mutual thing we shared between us, *death*.

"*Here is a call for the endurance of the saints, those who keep the commandments of God and their faith in Jesus.*" My mother said, sitting me on her lap. "Ara, are you listening?"

I looked at her wrist that was bandaged up. She had just been released from the hospital two days ago. My father, who was at work, didn't want to leave her side but she insisted he go.

"I'm listening." I said, resting my head on her shoulder. I liked hearing her voice as she read things to me.

"I heard you and Charlotte playing the other day." She paused. "You called her your wife?"

I smiled. "We liked to pretend we're married sometimes."

"A marriage belongs to a man and woman." She sounded constricted, as if she was straining her voice not to yell. And then she was crying hysterically. In sudden fear, I got up and ran to my room. That's when the front door opened, my father's work boots hitting the floor as I heard pages being torn from what could only be my mother's book.

"What the hell is going on? Where's Ara?" My father asked.

"*The devil prowls around...*" She said, as if it were a secret.

"Do you want me to call 911 again?" My father murmured. I peeked around the doorframe. My mother was now pacing, running her hands through her thick hair.

"Did you know about Charlotte and Ara?" She hissed. "They plan to marry."

"They're just kids." My father said, catching my eye.

"*They shall surely be put to death; their blood is upon them.*"

"I told you, if you continue to spew that bullshit in our home, I will leave with Ara." He shouted. I closed the door to my bedroom, crawling into my bed to hide beneath my covers. Later that night, I felt a hand on my forehead as I slept. I opened my eyes. My mother, standing over me, bent down and whispered, "I'm sorry." I invited her to lay next to me, like we always used to do when I was much younger.

"Ara..." She said, after I began to drift off. "When the end of the world comes, be ready to answer to Him."

"What happens when the world ends." I asked, eyes still closed. My mother then described something so monstrous and so chilling, I still feel the hair raise on my arms to this very day.

"Was your mother always so...religious?" Solene asked,

cautiously. We were laying in a tangled mess on top of the bed sheets, still slick with the sweat from the heat of the moment.

"My mother almost died giving birth to me. She said I tore her apart from the inside out." I paused. "The near death experience led her to God. But when the postpartum psychosis hit, my mother became obsessed."

"Tell me more about your mother." Solene insisted.

"What would you like to know?"

"Do you look like her?"

"I do. At least that's what my father says."

"I look just like my mother." Solene said proudly, but there was a sadness behind her eyes. I smiled, tracing the curve of her nose.

"Do you believe in Judgement day?" I asked, glancing at the window. It was two in the morning. I could see the tall buildings' silhouettes and the glow from the street lamps down below.

"I was told it was *The promise and threat*. We rarely spoke of it when I was little, but I knew about it. I knew of the resurrection of dead bodies… I used to believe, I really did. But Ara, I don't want to believe anymore if it means I can't be with you."

I gripped her hand as she buried her face into my chest. I attempted to breathe softly. I could still hear my mother's words that have now shaped every dream since Solene's arrival. I could still hear her wailing from the next room over as my father begged her to stop. And I could not help but know what she would say to me now, as I lay in bed with another woman.

"Don't let this ruin us." She pleaded.

I was ready to tie my entire existence to hers.

"I think you were meant only for me, like a rib taken from my side."

"You can't just say *I love you*?" Solene said, grinning.

"I never really knew how to love gently." I said, kissing her fiercely. I was ready for her to crack open my chest, to see the heart that beats for her, to see the lungs that breathe for her. I was so restlessly in love, for I knew I could never put it into words.

My mother's funeral happened on a sunny day. The sun felt vulgar in light of the events to unfold. They lowered her casket into the ground and I watched it the whole way down. My father clutched my shoulder. I was the one who took care of him, now. I made him eat, made him *still* take care of me. But somewhere along the way, he gave up. I'll never forget the words of the pastor. *We therefore commit the body to the ground.* Because, even though it had already been days without her, I had now just come to the realization she was *gone*. Gone in the way that insects will eat her. Gone in a way I could not fully fathom as a ten year old child. And after everything, after all her bible verses and her sanctity, I found out through the internet that she didn't even make it to heaven. With one simple search, I read that my mother had committed a mortal sin. Hamlet's vacilation. Virginia with her pocket of stones. Plath's head in the oven. I knew better than to question my mother's actions. I just couldn't help but think, *what was the point of it all?*

We spent the night wide awake. Four a.m. passed and then soon six a.m. came along, and still we made no effort to stop. Confessions, deep secrets, making love, we did it all in the span of hours. Solene spoke of Iraq like it was a place we could return to together, yet she made it clear it was just a fantasy of hers. There was no going back, she said. I knew more about her than I knew of myself, which made me crazy in ways I could never explain.

"I never talk about him, but I had a brother." Solene said, closing the curtains to hide the morning light so we could reside in this darkness just a little while longer. She continued on, "His name was Saleh. He was only seventeen years old when he was murdered."

"You can talk about him with me, if you want to."

Solene smiled, "He made me laugh until my stomach hurt. Saleh was the life of the party. Now I can hardly remember his laugh."

I kissed the back of her hand and let the silence speak for itself. Within the silence, she knew just how sorry I was we both had to strain to remember our dead family. My mother's smile, though rare, was slipping from my memory.

"Do you think it goes away?" Solene said, watching our hands twine.

"The grief?"

"Yes, the grief."

"I'm still trying to figure that out." I said, knowing that wasn't the answer she wanted. "I think, with time, grief just gets pushed down. Suppressed. But never extinguished."

"Please, never leave me. I don't think I can endure it." She whispered.

"Solene, I could never leave you."

"How do you know... How do you know I'm good for you?"

"There's just something about you..." I paused. "You remind me who I am."

"And who is that?" She asked.

"Someone who is happy to be alive."

It was vivid, the day my father took me to therapy for the first time. My mother claimed therapy was a hoax. But amid her own sadness, she failed to see mine. I was nine years old. Afraid of heights and confused by the bottomless pit that was my chest, too heavy to carry my own breathing, I had panic attacks that left me empty. The therapist asked how my home life was. I said it was good. I talked about my father and his caring nature. When she asked about my mother, I looked down at my hands and said she never left her bed, but when she did, she had this way about her. What do you mean, the therapist would ask. It was as if she were sleep walking. My father would sometimes spoon feed her. She was agitated and then crying all in the same breath. I feel as though our home is haunted. Why is that? Because the air is cold and her anger is demonic. I don't mean to speak that way about my mother, but it was maddening to know I was subjected to this at such a vulnerable age. Are you happy? I don't know how to answer that. Afterwards, on the drive home, my father asked how it went. I shrugged. And with a lump in my throat I dreaded walking through the front door. *I don't know how to answer that.* There wasn't an answer in this world to encapsulate the feeling of not wanting to be alive.

Chapter nine

Out, brief candle

It was just like any other day. Without much sleep, we ordered room service. I wrote in my journal while drinking a cup of coffee with two sugars and one cream. Solene asked what I was writing and I blushed. I was compiling and composing this journal into a poetry book dedicated solely to her. I handed her the journal timidly, and watched her eyes absorb the page one word at a time.

"Ara, this is..." Solene began.

"Cheesy? Lame? Embarrassing?"

"Romantic. I've never had someone write about me. Let alone write about me so beautifully. You have a gift."

I took the journal back and hid my face in my cup of coffee. I didn't take compliments well. "Thank you." I finally said.

"I can just picture you becoming this world renowned poet once we're in New York."

I climbed onto her, tasting the coffee in her mouth.

"What do you want to do today?" She asked, kissing me back.

I looked at the clock. It was now ten a.m. Strangely enough, I didn't feel tired. I felt energized and reborn, not worn down to the bone. A confessional was all I needed to patch up my fatigue, as if it were a gaping hole. I summoned back the memory of last night when Solene said *If you want blood, I will give it to you*. I told her we can barter in blood to make a pact.

"Trevi Fountain. Let's go." I said, patting her back, making an attempt to get out of bed. We were still naked, our skin sticky with sweat. She pulled me back onto the mattress, ambushing me with an array of kisses. It was tempting. But we couldn't be locked in here forever, no matter the bliss that came with it. Solitude was growing to be our language.

"Come on, we can shower together. We're a mess." I laughed.

"Why the rush?"

She could count on me to tell the truth but I wasn't sure she wanted to hear it.

"I want to be with you. Actually be with you. Out there." I motioned to the window.

"I'm trying." Solene said, closing her eyes and throwing an arm over her face. Her anguish was an art. Her sculpted form, a masterpiece.

With the little time we had left in the day to be intimate, I got onto my knees in the shower and buried my face between her legs. Her noises, stifled and voracious, I felt her hands in my wet hair. She washed my body once I was done. Lathering my breasts with soap, she dissected me with her hands and I sprung open like a flower. If she wanted to choose seclusion over *us*, I would let her.

"My grandmother is sick again." Solene said, walking back into our room with a look of concern.

"Should we stay?"

"She said it's just a cold."

"Let's stay."

"She insists we should go without her."

"We can ask room service to check on her."

"Good idea." Solene said, her braid laying over her shoulder. I was the one who braided her hair, kissing each strand as I tied them together. "Let's ride bikes to the fountain. It's not too far from here."

Dappled with ferocity and lamenting, days turned incoherent. My father took a drink one week after my mother's death and then chose to never stop. I didn't understand his actions, the way he slurred and stumbled. The way he cried in his empty room while I pressed my ear to the door to listen. Was something wrong with me? I hadn't cried yet. I was painless. I turned eleven. I wrote in my first journal. I got my period. I learned that death did not pause time, no matter the amount of stillness that came with it. And on the first day of sixth grade, I met Samantha. When asked about the absence of a mother, I said *I just didn't have one*. Samantha didn't push me for a better answer. I knew then she was going to be my escape. We made friendship bracelets, shared Junie B Jones books, and ate dinner at her house almost every night. Her family took me in with open arms. But when it grew dark and I had to go back home, I almost begged them to let me stay. My father would always be waiting for me in the front room, glued to the couch, flipping through channels with a lifeless stare. I was greeted with crossness. With urges to tell him to be a real father, to clean himself up, I instead mourned him in private.

"Why don't we ever go to your house?" Samantha asked.

"My house is haunted." I simply said.

Samantha laughed and continued on with the puzzle we were doing. It wasn't until we were much older, when my father chased me out into the yard when I backtalked him, did Samantha finally understand.

It was just like any other day. Riding our bikes on the cobblestoned streets, I let the warm air swarm me like a hug. After our long night of revelations and oaths, I watched her differently. I watched her as if she would disappear into thin air. She rode ahead of me, sticking her arms out wide as she pedaled fast. I was stiff with terror. The thought of losing her was insurmountable. She shared things with me that I will carry for the rest of my life. I can't bear to have that as the only thing to remember her by. I shared things too, things that I never thought I'd pull from myself like ribbons. My heatwave of suffering became a forest fire. Could we happily burn together?

We stood on a corner, lost. Solene didn't have any service so we attempted to ask strangers passing by for directions. No one knew English.

"Trevi Fountain?" Solene said, taking out a tourist pamphlet to show the picture. The man understood, pointing ahead and walking forward, we pushed our bikes to follow.

"Grazie." Solene said, once we arrived. The man nodded, waving his goodbye. We now stood at the junction of three roads, admiring the fountain before us, surrounded by baroque architecture. We walked down the steps to get a closer look, navigating through the endless crowds of people who stood around. Solene was now close enough to jump in. I almost wanted to dare her. I stepped closer to look at the litter of coins spread out along the bottom. Each coin glistened while the sun beat down on me.

"Everything seems so soft."

"Soft?" Solene said, hands resting on the marble as she hunched over to watch the water glisten.

"You soften the world."

Solene stood up straight and looked at me with her usual fear. The fear of being caught. She corrected her face immediately as if it was a bad habit.

"I know what you mean."

"You do?"

"You alleviate the deepest of my wounds."

I hope she knows she has *almost* healed me. She has stitched up each cut with such precision. I was in debt to her.

"Solene, I can't picture a life without you."

I made a simple prayer in my head for the skeletons in my closet to let this last. Solene inched closer. The crowds of people and their loud conversation had now become overwhelming.

"Don't picture it." She said, rubbing her thumb across my cheek. "Just *be* here with me."

"What are you doing?" I murmured.

"I'm *being* here with you." She said, tilting her head to meet my mouth. I gave in. There were dozens of people around us, we were not in our bedroom, the world might end, and still she kissed me so deeply I could feel gravity holding us there. Time slowed down. The tourists vanished and the fountain's waterfall was the only sound. And then she stopped, stepping away from me slowly. I looked around to realize no one was even paying attention. We had gone unnoticed. Not a single person here cared if two girls shared a kiss. I closed my eyes again, breathing in and out the humid air.

"Was that alright?" Solene asked. I opened my eyes. She was smiling. I smiled back at her, trying to communicate my new perspective of *Loving you doesn't have to be a hiding place when the apocalypse comes.*

"That was..."

"Crazy. Right?"

I began to laugh as she joined in. The laughter carried on as I took her into my arms, hugging her with a sense of deprivation. Our laughter drifted off with a sigh. She reached for my hand, taking me back up the steps and to our bikes that we had left in an alleyway. We slow danced to live music that played nearby. We kissed against the stone wall. We were deliriously content and I really thought even the memory of this would be forever rooted in happiness. I was wrong.

It was just like any other day. We rode our bikes, away from the city, for what seemed like hours. Standing at the edge of a field, I put down my kickstand and gulped down half my water bottle.

"Even as friends, it felt good to be with you." Solene said suddenly.

Did it feel good for me, I thought. I was grateful for her friendship. But I don't think I could do it all over again. I felt sick just thinking of laying in bed in her hoodie, smelling the cinnamon as I touched myself. All this turmoil, from the beginning, turned out to be a lovelorn child wearing a sheet. I was haunted by my own perception, skewed by trauma.

"I don't think I could ever *just* be your friend, Solene." I said, defeated.

"I don't want to be the girl who is just another poem in the books you write."

I told her she was the entire narrative of an idyllic life I'd like to write. She kissed me, hard. I kissed her back to quench my thirst. Plath claimed to be *pathetically intense. I just can't be any other way.* I knew I couldn't be any other way even if I tried. Solene walked to the nearest tree in the field and sat down as I followed.

"I miss you when I sleep." She admitted.

"I miss you even when you're *here*, beside me." I said,

laying on my side in the dry grass to face her. "I would call you Eurydice, in my head. My Eurydice. A single glance over my shoulder and you're gone."

"I'm here. I'm not going anywhere." Solene said.

"There's no guarantee in the finality of love."

Solene pursed her lips, deep in thought. I didn't mean to make it all about me and my careless need to display my insecurities.

"Have faith in me."

It wasn't about faith. It was about heartache. Like clockwork, I couldn't deny it came each time to demolish me for sport.

"Faith isn't this holy thing..."

"Ara, just let me care for you." She said, frustrated.

"I'm still in the room where my mother died. I don't know how to leave." I paused, "I don't mean to be obstinate in your attempt to pull me out."

"I'll be patient."

I swear, I loved her. As was the beauty of Orpheus' lyre, I knew I could never look back.

It was just like any other day. And this was the *day*, in the heated evening, that I gave my tirade against all who did not favor us. We were now in a bookstore, shuffling through piles of used books, giggling, when Solene stopped to look at me.

"This doesn't mean I'm coming out to my grandmother."

"I never said you should."

"And you'll be okay with that?"

"I have to be." I shrugged.

"See. There it is."

"What?"

"You're being passive aggressive."

"What else am I supposed to say?"

"Would you come out to your mom if she was still alive?"

I inhaled sharply and glanced down at the book in my hands. I already knew what my mother would say. I've played it over in my head until I was blue in the face.

"I wouldn't." I said, "But she would've found out."

"My grandmother won't find out."

"Okay." I was done with the conversation. Solene knew I was mad and to my surprise she took my face in her hands, right in between the poetry and playwright section, and kissed me.

"I'm sorry." She sighed. I sighed too. We continued skimming through the books as I was now set afire, touching my bottom lip. Whether it be in a room or at a fountain full of strangers, sharing our most intimate moments was riveting. If I ever etched misery into my soul after times like these, it was only due to future circumstances. Never the present. In the present I was sound of mind, content and fulfilled. If I ever woke up in the night screaming and thrashing, it was only due to what was to come. Never this *moment*. Her rind, I'd like to taste. Bold and compelling. I'd

147

kill to eat. In her entirety. I loved her. *Listen, to the way I went on and on.* But tragedy was coming.

It was just like any other day. Night had fallen by the time we returned to the hotel. I was exhausted. The air was different, as though a layer of dust had settled around us.

"I'm going to check on my grandmother." Solene said. "See you back in the room."

I wanted to fall instantly into bed. I went to take a shower instead, closing my eyes when the hot water poured onto me. I was sunburnt and sore. It was a Tuesday. I counted the days on my fingers. I looked down to see blood run down into the drain. My period had come. No wonder I was so capricious. *No guarantees.* I rolled my eyes and continued to wash my body. After I got out, dried off and brushed my hair; I realized Solene was still gone. I thought nothing of it, reaching for my journal to write about the day. *Was it too much to love this way*, I wrote. I answered, *Eros gave me permission.* My hand began to cramp after I filled pages. I eventually rolled onto my back to stare at the ceiling out of boredom. Where was Solene? I could watch a movie, finish reading my book, or just wait in silence. I waited for quite some time. Waited with anticipation, to have Solene walk right through that door. I lounged across the bed like a nude painting. She never seemed to care when I was on my period. *We can just put a towel down.* I smiled. I observed my nails that I so desperately wanted to bite. It was a nervous habit. It would drive my mother up the wall. I was a nervous child. Always walking on eggshells. I sighed, standing up at last to find clothes to put on. I was going to check on Vinos and Solene. It was nearly midnight. I grabbed the key card and walked down the hallway. I hovered outside the door, worried I was barging in on a private family matter. I knocked. Seconds passed and then the door creaked open.

"Ara?"

"Is everything okay?"

"Please, help me." Her voice sounded broken. I slid through the crack of the door and immediately Solene collapsed into me.

"Solene..." I glanced around, my eyes landing on Vinos, who was lying in bed with her eyes closed.

"She's dead, she's dead." Solene said, shaking in my arms.

"What do you mean dead? Vinos, wake up!" I went over to the bed and gently shook her. She was still warm. I felt my insides stiffen. "Wake up!"

"Ara, be quiet."

"Why haven't you called the police? What the fuck." I covered my face. This was a dream. A sick dream.

"Look at me." Solene said, grabbing my arms with authority. "If we call the police, your father will find us."

I shook my head frantically. "No, this isn't right. We have to call them." I pulled away from her grasp and began to pace.

"I'm trying to help you." Solene implored.

"This isn't helping. This is barbaric." I was now close

to tears. I couldn't stop staring at Vinos' lifeless body.

"I love my grandmother, but she would want you to be safe from your father."

"What do you suggest? We leave her here?" I scoffed.

"No. We'll leave her somewhere that won't connect her to us." Solene whispered.

"Oh god." I said, sliding to the ground.

"We've come too far to give up." Solene cried. "Your father will take you from me."

"That doesn't justify..."

"Do this for me." She said, kneeling down to where I was sitting on the floor.

"I'm almost eighteen..."

"Do you think if you go home we'd ever see each other again?"

"I don't know." I whispered, mournfully.

"I'm not taking that chance. I can't lose you."

I was forged into her, beaten to a pulp by obsession. I know this now to be a dangerous obsession. I considered what she was saying.

"Okay." I said, just quiet enough that I wasn't sure she heard me. Solene pulled me in, clinging to me as if I was the grief she had not yet processed. I then watched her walk over to the bed and kiss Vinos' forehead. I couldn't bear to continue to look. This was hell, if anything. Maybe the world did end. We were murderers, if nothing.

Chapter ten

Sacrificial lamb

It began in my backyard with a stone in hand. The girl on the other side of the fence was goading me, claiming I couldn't help build her fort. The brutal stars I saw instead of blue sky was troubling. I clenched the rock in my fist and spoke to her through the hole in the wood. She laughed at my obvious desperation to be liked. It began, the evil, *that very evil of being antagonized until you see red*. It began when she asked for that rock. I crossed my arms in defeat as I surrendered it, carelessly hurling it over the fence with all my strength. I heard a loud thump, a high pitched scream, and sudden gurgling. I peeked through the hole in the fence. I saw the neighbor girl on the ground, bleeding profusely into the grass. I felt my heart push up into my throat as I bolted through the yard, into the house, and under my bed. I hid there until I heard a knock. It was the front door. Soft voices exchanged conversation and then my dad was calling my name. I wept until he found me. He pulled me out from under the bed and demanded to know why I hurt Michelle. I wept and wept and then he was hugging me. Michelle had stitches in her head when I saw her in dance class a week later. Those brutal stars never came and went again. I never saw red again. I never wished to kill. I never even wished her harm despite my anger. Yet my cruelty that day felt like an awakening. My craziness, self inflicted. My obsessiveness, always a weapon. It began in my backyard with a stone in hand.

We put the *do not disturb* sign on her bedroom door. Vinos was now gone. Our bliss had atrophied, dispersed into ruins. And then I felt sick for blaming her death for ending *our* paradise. Was I really so selfish? Was my sincerity a hoax? I watched Solene pace the room.

"It will be fine." She said, most likely to herself. She was in a dreamlike, manic state. I, on the other hand, was painfully aware. Languorous and scathing, I was a myth. I was an exit wound. *Solene, did you know my heart aches for you in unimaginable ways?*

"We should get some sleep." I said, clearing my throat. It hadn't been that long since we had found Vinos but it felt like hours had passed. Still dark outside, I could feel my eyes growing heavy. I couldn't imagine waking up without Vinos there to greet us.

"We can't sleep until we move her." Solene stated. I was glad we were back in our own room. I couldn't be near a dead body without thinking of my mother. I was reliving my grief all at once.

"Okay." I murmured. I wasn't ready to argue. I was ready to let this be over.

"You must think I'm a monster." Solene said.

"I just don't understand. Explain to me why we have to leave her?" My voice cracked on the last word and then Solene was on her knees in front of me.

"I don't want to. I don't want to." She chanted, "But I also don't know what will happen if we go back to America. Running away might not be illegal in California but how will your father react? What if he actually hits you this time? What if..." She starts to cry. I put my arms around her, kissing her face.

"Okay." I said, firmly. "Whatever you want. I will do it."

"Thank you." She whispered. I didn't know what she was thanking me for. For vowing to discard the only known family member she had left? For cleaning up what is now considered to be a crime scene? I didn't want her *thank you*. I wanted it to go back to the way it was.

"So we'll just hide her body?" I asked.

"Yes."

"And everything will be okay?"

"Yes."

"I'm scared." I hated to admit it.

"Me too."

"How do you do it?"

"Do what?" Solene said, calmly.

"Hide fear so well?"

"When I found my family... I had never known fear like that. Nothing has ever come close. At least I know my grandmother died peacefully. At least I know I have you."

I didn't want to say *What if she didn't die peacefully? In pain and all alone. And yes you have me, but what if you wake up one day and realize I'm not enough?* So instead I say,

"You have me, Solene. Until the very end." She kissed me and I kissed her back with the fear I never tried to hide. We went back to not talking. Just sitting on opposite ends of the room, the T.V. playing in the background. I eventually broke the silence as the minutes passed, I couldn't stand it.

"Where will we put her?"

"I don't know."

"How will we move her?"

"I don't know."

"How will..."

"Just stop!" Solene exclaimed, rubbing at her temple. "Ara, I know just as much as you."

"Solene..." I began cautiously.

"Don't. Don't try to talk me out of it. I've made up my mind. I'm doing this to save you." She sounded frantic and dissociated from the person I knew as *Solene.*

"Fine."

Solene stood from where she was sitting on the floor and eyed my suitcase that laid open. Walking over to the luggage, she began to throw out my clothes and sat down in it before I could object. My blood ran cold when I realized what she was doing.

"No." I whispered.

"Do you have a better suggestion?"

I didn't say anything so she went back to sizing up the suitcase by curling in a ball and laying down. She fit perfectly. Vinos was smaller than her. Vinos too would fit perfectly. I was sick just picturing it.

"Solene, get out."

"Ara..."

"Get out." I said through gritted teeth. I covered my face, attempting to hide my sudden rage. Solene got out immediately and took me into her arms, I pulled away. She wouldn't allow it. I fought back.

"Ara, calm down."

"Why don't you care?"

"Care about what?"

"About her? She's dead!"

"You don't think I care? She was my grandmother. She was all I had left." Solene said, now being the one to push me away.

"I didn't mean that. I just think that you're in shock..."

"I'm doing this for you!" She shouted. I had never heard her voice raise to such a level. I stared back in disbelief.

"I never asked you to do this..."

"Call the police then. You're free to do so. I'm not holding you hostage." Solene said, folding her arms. Staring at each other for quite some time, I didn't move a single inch. I didn't even make an attempt to reach for the phone next to me. Solene took that as my answer and picked up the suitcase.

"I can do this part alone." Solene said, walking to the door.

"I can help." I said, ashamed at how I let this love overtake me. How I let it riddle me with mistakes that will forever haunt me. We walked back to Vinos' room calmly.

Once inside, Solene set the suitcase down and placed a white sheet over Vinos' body. We said nothing to one another as we lifted her up and set her inside the suitcase. Solene was the one who moved to form her body to fit. I just watched with a blank stare. After zipping it shut, Solene put her knees to her chest and asked me to leave the room. I left without a word. It took several tries to get back into our room as I kept dropping the key card. My hands were shaking furiously. I was as stiff as plywood. I stood in the middle of the room. I looked at the time. I could write in my journal. I could watch T.V. I could read. But all of that felt hollow. In the face of death, nothing felt worthwhile. Thirty minutes had passed when Solene came back, eyes dull and lifeless.

"We'll leave the suitcase as far away from here as possible." She said, her voice surprisingly steady.

"And?"

"I'll figure out the rest."

"You don't have to figure it out all on your own."

"You want nothing to do with this. You've made that very clear."

I didn't respond, but I did go up to her and kiss every inch of her face to make up for my resistance.

"Ara, I need you." She murmured.

"I need you too."

Our words must've had different meanings because Solene was suddenly ripping into me, leading me over to the bed and laying me down before I could comprehend what was happening.

156

"I can't, Solene. I can't." I said, sitting up. Solene looked at me with utter betrayal.

"Let me forget. Please."

"I can't."

Silence fell. It was time for us to stow the suitcase. *How did we let it get this far?*

"Do you think about death?"

It was a Sunday night. I was fourteen, and I closed my eyes tight in hope of disappearing.

"I'm afraid of death." Samantha said.

"Me too." I lied. I never told Samantha how my mother passed away because it wasn't something I told people. No matter who it was. But in this moment I almost said, *sometimes I feel like my mother's suicide normalized death for me. Sometimes I feel like her death is something I will inherit, like a gift.*

"Why do you ask?" Samantha said, closing her textbook. It was nearing the end of the school year and we were eager for summer break.

"Just wondering."

"Okay." She didn't press me further and we continued to study. We were at her house so my father was not something I had to worry about. Yet the nagging sensation of misery was still present. I'd still have to go home. I'd still have thoughts about death and continue to tell no one. I'd still have to coexist with a body that did not want me. Girlhood was rejecting me. I was misplaced by rage. Why should I make an effort for a future I will probably destroy? My attempt at life was up in flames. I was wandering through those flames, eyeless and disoriented. I wanted nothing more than my gift, now.

Chapter eleven

Child of Cain

I wanted to be swallowed whole. I wanted to be utterly devoured until the vessels of my marrow and my bare bones consolidated with hers. But it was never supposed to happen like this. *I can't exist without you.* Her words flooded my diaphragm. I had a coughing fit when I said it back. *Not like this, not like this.* We left Vinos at a nearby fire station. I could not and will not forget her voice as she repeated بيبي اشوفج بالجنة بيبي. الله يرحمج over and over, hugging the suitcase close to her. I never wished to know what it meant. I ran down the alleyway until I could no longer suppress it. With one hand on the brick and the other holding back my hair, I threw up until I was empty. Solene was still clinging to the suitcase, crying.

"We have to go before someone sees us." I said, appearing next to her when I knew I was calm enough. It was the early morning, the streets were barren. "No, I can't leave her." She wailed. Her hands, trembling.

"Be quiet." I whispered, gently.

"Grandmother, I love you. Wake up. Wake up."

"Solene, we can't be seen here."

"I can't leave her." She repeated. I put both hands on her shoulders and tugged her hard. She resisted, but soon enough clung to me instead. How could both of us ever be okay again? The brutal way we were abandoning Vinos. The brutal way this love was growing into something venomous. I failed to find the antidote.

Sucking down a breath of Rome's humid air, I thought of screaming. I then thought of my mother in her casket. They put too much blush on her. I stood close enough to see the foundation caked on. She never wore makeup when alive, so it didn't make sense to me. When it was just my father and I in the church, he broke down over her body. It was the first time I had ever seen him cry. He was crying like a child. I was mesmerized by his vulnerable display. Was death the true catalyst for love? Because it seemed like my parents' marriage was volatile. That wasn't true, it couldn't be. I remembered the way they danced in the kitchen. I remembered when my mother begged my father to kill her. I could go back and forth in my mind, but it would always just come back to where he draped himself over her corpse, cursing the god he did not believe in.

"Don't look at me like that." Solene said. We were back at the hotel, packing our belongings in a hurry. It was almost dawn.

"I'm not looking at you."

"We did a terrible thing. But we did it for each other." Solene said, "You're looking at me like I committed..."

"A crime? It's because *we* did." I snapped.

"For each other." She said, slowly.

I couldn't blame her. I was her willing accomplice. *For each other.* How could I ever second guess the intention of her devotion? I took her hand and twined our pinkies, kissing them. I was sealing our fate. I didn't know what I was in for with just *one* pinky promise.

"I have a friend in Barcelona." Solene said. "Taking the train there will be more discreet. I looked it up, it's a little over seventeen hours."

At the train station I was paranoid. I felt like everyone was staring as if they knew what we did. We sat on the bench after purchasing tickets, I rested my head on Solene's shoulder and closed my eyes. I hadn't slept in well over thirty hours. I never wanted to sleep again. I could already feel the nightmares creeping in. Vinos' color drained from her face at the Colosseum. Did she know right then? She died all alone. Did she suffer? An enormous wave of despair collisions into me. I wanted my mom. I wanted my dad. I could leave Solene, crawl back to my father, and hope the abuse gets better. *But* I knew I could never leave, I'd miss her too much. I'd probably die from the absence of her. *The absence of her in my ribcage that encases her.* That was reason enough to stay.

Boarding the train, we sat at the very back. I couldn't feel the calamitous weight of our actions hit quite yet. I didn't know what it would feel like when it did. Solene gripped my thigh and I found no reassurance in it. I looked at her. She must have seen the dejection all over my face, because she cupped my cheek and kissed me in a way that pleaded with my veins to detangle themselves from misery.

161

There had to be intention behind this, behind it all.

"This is why I have to believe." Solene said, "I have to believe that I will see my grandmother in heaven."

"I know." I looked to the sky out the window of the train and still, I felt hopeless. I will never see my mother again and she will never see Vinos. Death to me was never easy, but the definiteness was comforting. I never had to think *Will they be walking through that door?* because I knew death meant forever.

"I'm not evil. I swear." Solene whispered. I didn't know if she was talking to herself or to me. I kissed her. She wiped away the tears that pooled in her eyes.

"I know." I repeated.

After the second train transfer, I really needed to sleep. I looked in the bathroom mirror and saw how red my eyes were. My face, puffy. Solene and I fell asleep with our heads pressed together. I was calmed by the motion of the train. We were now miles and miles away from Vinos' body. Somebody had to have found her by now. Maybe they thought *What kind of monster would leave her here?* My dreams that day were cyclical. Vinos was in her house knitting. She spoke of Iraq and its beauty. She was speaking in English as she described the tall green trees that hid beyond the desert. And then the image morphed before me. Solene was under the orange tree, asking me to quote something to her. *I like the way you know so much.* She said. I quoted Carson. *What next? What next if we are to survive this?* She didn't like that one. I racked my mind for the perfect one. She grew impatient. *What lived and died between us haunts me.* Yuknavitch's words hung in the air like a deadly prognosis. The image morphed again, the orange tree fading. A covered figure stood in my room. I approached it, pulling off the sheet, revealing a doleful Vinos. Her skin was cold and pale, her mouth opened like Munch's scream. I sat up in my seat, hyperventilating. I was awake. The man a few rows over looked at me with concern.

"What happened?" Solene mumbled, stirring awake as I tried to calm my heart.

"Just a dream. Go back to sleep."

"Ara..."

"I need to get off this train."

"We still have hours until the next transfer."

I have bled more than this and I will bleed more again. I repeated it like an affirmation. I didn't feel rested. Do the cursed ever sleep? I adjusted myself in my seat. And then I readjusted again. Solene put a hand on my knee to calm me.

"Don't." I said, standing up to walk to the bathroom. The train shook me as I splashed cold water onto my face. I cried silently, for just a few minutes, before slapping myself. Not hard, but just enough to snap out of it. How does one snap out of a depth as deep as sorrow? Was I now just a placeholder for grief, a space for constant mourning? Shakespeare was right. *Everyone can master a grief but he that has it.*

I walked back out once I knew I could contain myself. Solene was waiting, her brow furrowed with stress. She was the one who had lost a grandmother. How could I be so selfish?

"I'm sorry." I said, sitting down to take her hand. I was letting her know I was *here*.

"We'll get through this." She said, "احبك" I smiled for the first time in what felt like days. I've lost track of time. I responded but, now, I can't recall for the life of me what I said.

At the train station in Barcelona, I walked off the platform and turned to Solene. She was standing in place, suitcase beside her. I knew there was a war raging inside her. Now an orphan, every single family member ripped from her savagely. I could feel it raging from where I stood. I could feel it when we got to the hotel. I felt it inside her mouth, I felt it in my fingertips that danced their way across her hips, and I felt it thrum through her bloodstream like a song.

"We can stop." I said.

"I don't want to." She said, initiating another kiss while undressing. I tried to ignore the wetness of her tears against my skin. *I tried.*

"Solene, stop."

Solene then broke down and I held her tight. To be like Patroclus going headstrong into battle sporting Achilles' armor, I wanted to take her place, to save her. But she was not a damsel and we were not a myth. Foolish and reckless is what we might be. I could taste the salt of her tears. I swore she was the sea. Her ebb and flow, calming. But even seas had their storms.

In the morning we met up with her friend, Layla, at a cafe. She and Solene went to school together and stayed in contact for all these years when Solene left Iraq. Layla was tall, taller than Solene, with broad shoulders and short brown hair.

"Nice to finally meet you." She said, "Solene won't shut up about you." I never asked Solene what Layla thought we were.

"Nice to meet you too." I said.

"You two can stay with me as long as you want. I heard you're traveling for the summer?"

"Yeah, so far only Rome."

"What does Vinos think about this?" Layla smiled. "I know she used to keep you on a short leash."

Solene clenched her jaw. We hadn't gone over what we'd say if someone brought up her grandmother. Solene leaned forward to take a sip of her coffee.

"Vinos is happy for me." Solene smiled, showing too much teeth.

"Good. So tell me all about Rome."

At Layla's apartment, she apologized for the size, showing us to the tiny guest room that could only fit a double bed.

"Hope you two don't mind sleeping in the same bed." Layla laughed. I laughed, a little too hotly.

"It's perfect. Thanks again for letting us crash with you." Solene said. "I think I need a nap. That train ride was rough."

Layla excused herself from the room, mentioning something about running a few errands. Solene locked the door, falling onto the bed with a groan. I laid down next to her, watching her face drown in the afternoon light. The window was open. I could hear people existing down on the street.

"I used to tell Layla that my grandmother was the only one who could keep me sane." Solene murmured, "I loved my mom, but my grandma was the one who understood me most."

"I can keep you sane."

"No, you can't." Solene said, kissing me. "You drive me crazy."

I knew what she meant. She stirred up something inside me that felt like torment. I kissed her back and then we fell into a deep sleep.

Isn't there always something we want more than our own happiness? A pull toward the fall. Haven't we all loved too much? I read Danusha Lameris' words with a lump in my throat. Solene was still fast asleep, the sun was setting. Layla had not returned from running her errands. I closed the book with a sigh, tossing it aside as I felt Solene nestle into me. She sighed softly into my neck, draping an arm over my waist.

"Did I wake you?" I murmured.

"No." She said, her hand beginning to trail downward.

"Solene."

No answer. She was busy undoing the buttons of my pants. I wanted her. I did. But I felt she was not in her right mind.

"We shouldn't."

"Ara, please." She whispered, pulling me in. She pulled me in so sweetly, I could not resist. I propped up onto my elbows to watch her take off my pants, smiling as our eyes met. When she was done removing all that I was wearing, she kissed up my legs and to my thighs, obviously relishing in the small noises I made each time I felt her lips touch my skin. The front door opened with a loud thud. Layla was home.

"Hurry." Solene said, tossing me my clothes. "Hey Layla, we just woke up. We'll be right out."

"No problem." Layla shouted from down the hallway. I was dressed within seconds, giggling as Solene shook her head in mock horror. I took her into my arms and we kissed. I had this sense of belief that we were going to be okay.

We ate Chinese food that night, sitting on the floor of Layla's apartment. I was beginning to feel normal. I laughed at Layla's stories about Solene as a child. Solene seemed embarrassed, yet amused. I hoped she was feeling normal too. Even if it just lasted a few minutes, I hoped the pain allowed her to breathe in this moment. As we laughed, ate, and reminisced; I hoped she was safe from the guilt.

We were back in our own blissful bubble. Spain was now ours. But I never forgot Vinos, I never forgot her face.

But Solene refused to talk about it. She refused to even say her name, like it was taboo. I was trying my best to understand. I just couldn't wrap my mind around her way of coping. She took my clothes off every chance she got, kissing me as if she could find resolve within me. I willingly gave in each time. She was mourning. I wanted to give her everything. Whatever she wanted, she could have. And if it meant I became hollow in return, then so be it.

"There's a party tonight at Layla's friend's house." Solene said. We were both lying side by side, breathing heavily. Just minutes before, I was on top of her.

"Sounds fun." I said, that hollow feeling creeping up. It always came after the pleasure. And then we laid there in silence, not knowing what to say anymore because the reality was too much to bear.

The party was at a mansion. A giant four story modern day mansion with glass for walls. Just being in the house made me feel underdressed. I peered around to see everyone elegantly holding wine glasses and chatting in Spanish.

"This isn't the kind of party I had in mind." I murmured to Solene.

"Layla claimed this was a wild crowd." Solene said, "Let's go get a drink."

"Ara, Solene, come here!" Layla said, waving us over. "I wanted to introduce you to Tamara." And that's when I looked at the girl standing before me. Tamara. Her beauty, almost too intense to take in. Tamara held out her hand and shook Solene's. In return, Solene blushed. It was the way

Tamara let her hand linger. Her confidence was enticing.

"You two make a hot couple." Tamara said. Even her voice oozed lust.

"We're friends." Solene laughed.

"What a shame." She said, sipping on her wine glass. Eyes, a piercing dark blue.

"Where can I get a drink?" I asked. I was trying to pin down the anger I now felt towards Solene.

"I'll get you one." Tamara said, touching my shoulder. I glanced at Solene and she met my eyes, briefly, but just long enough to figure out I was irritated.

When Tamara appeared seconds later with a glass of red wine, I said thank you and excused myself to get some fresh air. The real party seemed to be outside. Dozens of people were in the pool, jumping off the diving board and splashing around with laughter. I downed my wine in a hurry, wiping my mouth with the back of my hand. I needed something stronger. I made my way over to the patio where they were playing beer pong. There was also an assortment of liquor bottles on a table. I snatched the tequila and poured half a glass into a red solo cup.

"I'm not going to just tell some random stranger that we're together." Solene said, appearing by my side.

"I get it."

"Do you?"

"Look, I want to get drunk. Do you want to get drunk?" I said, handing her a bottle. She took it from me with a smile. The night from there turned into something

169

promising. We drank nearly the entire bottle, wandering around the house to meet strangers and touching each other a little too fondly. When we walked back into the main room, where the music was now blaring, it was like walking into a completely different party. Several girls were kissing each other, the boys watched in awe.

"There you two are!" Tamara exclaimed. Even drunk, she seemed put together. I couldn't help but notice how she clung to Solene. Things were beginning to turn fuzzy, I was forgetting little details. I was tempted to take Solene's hand and let everyone know, including Tamara, that she was taken. I felt helpless. I felt helpless as Tamara took us to a nearby couch and talked to Solene in an animated manner.

"I'm from Sweden." Tamara said. They were going over every part of their lives together. But only I knew the true parts of Solene. I wasn't jealous. I was just bitter.

"What about you, Ara?"

"Hmmm?" I said, spacing out between each topic they ventured through.

"Are you single?"

"Yeah, I am." I smiled, vaguely.

"Just two single girls traveling Europe? I love it! We need to have some fun." Tamara said. Two brunettes were kissing opposite us. I needed to lie down.

"What kind of fun?" Solene said.

Was she flirting? I continued to drink from my cup despite the way my stomach turned.

"Here in Barcelona, we like to be friendly..." Tamara

said, scooting closer. Solene looked at me, her eyes said *I'm sorry* as Tamara leaned in, kissing her softly. They kissed for what seemed like an eternity. I was ready to get up and leave but Tamara finished the kiss and turned to me. I didn't even protest as she put her lips to mine. The inside of her mouth was warm and rich, I was completely entranced. She kissed differently than Solene. Different but still good. She pulled away and leaned back, implying it was mine and Solene's turn. I did so many things to keep us afloat, I turned myself inside and out. We both reached over Tamara to kiss. I kissed her with pent up frustration and so much love. Always giving myself away for love. Wearing myself down to the bone for love. Going back and forth, we all three shared each other for minutes at a time.

"We can find a room upstairs?" Tamara suggested. Solene shrugged and I glared at her. Tamara must have not felt tension because she took Solene's hand and kissed her once more.

"I'm sorry." I said, on the verge of breaking down. I stormed out of the room, out of the house, and realized I was stuck here. I had nowhere to go. I told myself I didn't care if Solene chose to go upstairs with Tamara. I didn't care what she did. I sat down on the steps, attempting to breathe evenly. I heard the front door open, the music traveling outward to the peaceful front yard.

"Ara." It was Solene.

"Don't." I realized I was crying now. "Go fuck her, I don't care."

"I don't want to." Solene said, sitting beside me. "I thought we were just having some fun."

"Kissing other girls is your idea of fun?"

"I'm sorry."

I stayed quiet, trying my best to keep my sobs lodged in my chest.

"We can go. I'll go get Layla." Solene said, gripping my shoulder before going back inside.

The ride home was awkward. Layla went on and on about Tamara. How they met, how great she was. I stayed silent in my own corner of the backseat, ignoring Solene's attempts at holding my hand. I never wished this on my worst enemy, the feeling of loving someone in secret. I wished I didn't love like I did. In such a faithful way that devoured me. I was faithful for the reason of wanting to be *wanted* in return. At Layla's apartment I went straight to bed, stripping down to just my underwear to feel the cool sheets against my skin. I was still drunk by the time Solene joined me. I was going to pretend I was asleep but it turns out *loving her* had no alternative. She climbed in bed, sliding under the sheets to press into me. I didn't have it in me to resist. Just like I couldn't resist when she inched her hand down the fabric of my underwear. I shuddered. I couldn't resist. I rolled onto her, kissing her with a forlorn moan. She moaned back, hands running through my hair. We didn't talk about Tamara after that. We made love numerous times that night, hushing each other when we got too noisy.

"You're mine." She whispered. And I thought *you're*

mine, you're mine. I'm going to keep you like an undying fire. And if I get burned, I will revel in the scars. I felt our sweat mingle and I knew there was no better feeling. I felt her hands shake while they took me apart and I knew this was a cure I'd seek out for the rest of my life.

"I feel like my happiness is temporary." Solene said. It was now four a.m. "I feel happy and then suddenly, it's all too much. It comes rushing into me."

"What comes rushing into you?"

"It's not sadness. More like the lack of any feeling." She whispered. I was hoping at that moment she would finally talk about Vinos. I was hoping she'd admit this was a result of all that we did, or rather all that we did not do. "You make me feel something." She said, and I now understood why the sex had become so constant. She was trying to maintain her last resemblance of emotion. I never chose to put an end to it because I was just as dependent.

The day drinking became a problem. I was annotating when suddenly Solene stepped into the room, obviously drunk by the way she swayed, mouth stained red from what could only be wine.

"Hi." She said, eyes wide with a sultry gaze.

"Hi." I murmured, setting my book aside. It was a humid day, my hair stuck to my forehead as I wished for any sort of breeze to come through the wide open window.

"Me and Layla were just out for lunch. I had too much wine." She said, falling onto the bed with a sigh.

"I can see that." I laughed.

"Read to me." She said, closing her eyes.

"You should take a nap. I can read to you later."

She frowned. I gazed at her with far too much affection because she took that as a sign to kiss me.

"Solene, not right now." Her mouth, sonorous against mine. I felt guilt for leading her astray. "Maybe later?" I added to cushion the rejection.

"Okay." She smiled, burrowing into me as she fell soundly asleep. I continued to read, highlighting and writing words in the margins for Solene to read later on. Mindy Nettifee said *one look from you and my spine reincarnates as kite string.* So I put: *For me, not kite string, but an elastic band that snaps back into any shape for you.* I was so caught up in Solene, I could hardly see that now I was a formless human who had no place to fit in.

Chapter twelve

Soothsayer

I knew when my mother was going to die before she did. My father would've known too if it weren't for the fact he was blinded by devotion. Even after her first attempt, he refused to believe that she was a danger to herself. He was weary when she was left alone, but he still saw her as the same woman he married right out of college. When he bathed her, fed her, and even dressed her, he still saw the woman he fell in love with. He didn't see a woman who belonged in a facility. Maybe that's romantic or maybe *for better or for worse* really did garner some truth. Maybe I was the one who was blinded. I knew when my mother was dead before I even opened her bedroom door. The pale shock on my father's face was genuine. I knew that he thought this could never happen. She could never leave him. But she did. She could never leave a daughter. But *she did*. And now I was the one who used her fate as a reflection of how my life was supposed to happen. *Everyone will eventually leave.*

Solene was disintegrating before me. Hardly speaking, only through touch. She would split me open each night, leaving me to clean up the mess. I forgave her. Countless times. But I had to forgive myself too. I made no attempt to save her. Made no attempt to stop her. Did I want her to stop? Was I just being cynical? What if this is just the happiest we'll ever be? As good as it's going to get, flesh and all. I was experiencing her in ways I never have before. In this boneyard of longing, I was buried deep.

"What are you thinking about?" Solene said. Her body was exposed to the moonlight. There was still the echo of laughter and music down on the street. Solene never spoke on nights like this. Not after we had sex, at least. We used to tell each other everything. I was now racing through my mind, nitpicking what to say.

"You." I settled with the truth.

"I think about you more than you'll ever know." She said, propping up on her arm to face me.

"Sometimes it doesn't seem that way." I said, cautiously.

"I know, I'm being selfish." She murmured. "I just don't know how to stop." We could have had a conversation right then and there. A *real* conversation. Yet I pulled her into me. I was just as ravenous. I was in this boneyard for life.

Solene didn't listen anymore. I talked about the weather and the news. I even talked about rewriting my life, asking her if she would like to be a part of it. She just stared, eyes vacant. I couldn't stand to see life die right out from under her like a fire put out by a cold wind. I was so desperate to have the old Solene back, I surrendered to her each time she decided to use me. She used me in a way that made me feel empty. An emptiness that ached alongside a love I thought I deserved. And I let her believe she was in the right. My mother talked about the righteous every day. My virtue was shrinking. She'd call me wicked and so I prayed that night for the first time in years. I knelt onto the floor, placing my elbows on the bed, and closed my eyes. Vinos' face is the first thing I saw. I prayed for her forgiveness. I heard the door to Layla's apartment open before I could continue on. I sprung up, embarrassed. I never held my own convictions, shaped by everyone who stepped foot in my life. I was a daughter, a friend, a partner. *Still* I was left with the symptom of what could only be diagnosed as agony. Solene walked into the room. I knew what she wanted.

"Drunk again?"

"Is that a problem?" She said, removing her shirt. I wanted everything from her. Down to the very bone, I wanted her. But I was also not oblivious, she wasn't herself.

"My father would drink..."

"Are you comparing me to your father?"

"No..."

"Not everyone who drinks is your father, Ara. I was just having some fun." She snapped, getting under the covers of the bed.

"You've been *having some fun* every night this week."

"I'm young, we're in Europe."

"Okay." I said.

"Okay?"

"I don't want to talk anymore."

"We don't have to talk." She murmured. I was tired but I reached for her body anyway. I was always willing to do the *one* thing that made us numb. I felt everything when she touched me, but the voices in my head became silent.

Therefore I became nothing. Just the embodiment of her escape.

My father never spoke to another woman after my mother died. He never went on any dates or got remarried. He never slept on my mother's side of the bed. He never learned to braid my hair. He never went to a support group for losing a loved one. He *never* made this house feel like a home. I didn't understand why he took me to her grave each day, only to watch him cry on the dead grass. I didn't understand why he threw things at the wall, as if anger would bring her back from the dead. I was taught that anger was a vessel for men to cope, when in reality anger was an intuitive thing that women must possess to survive. I *possessed* all the traits of my father, unwillingly. I survived off fury for the longest time. I was tied to wrath's organs, our wild nature conjoined. I dreamt of howling, black magic, and collecting bones. My mother, rarely, would speak of sorcery. Another sin in her eyes. But I wonder if she ever thought of me as a witch. Sometimes I'd feel so out of place in her eyes, I would hide away in my books and read about her so-called sins just to spite her. Was it spiteful if she never knew? *Will she ever know just how scared I was each time I gravitated toward those sins?*

"I can see your future."

"What does my future look like?"

"You're happy. You're a well known writer. And you

live in the city." Solene simply said, leaning back in her chair. The cafe was crowded. I kept my hands clasped around the hot mug of coffee, as if it wasn't eighty degrees outside. I tried to picture this vague life she drew up for me.

"What city?"

"Seattle, of course." She smiled.

I nodded, recalling the acceptance letter still in my bedside drawer. There was no time to wonder what a life would be like if I chose Seattle. I now had my eyes set on New York with Solene.

"What about your future? Can you see it?" I asked, watching her fidget in her chair. She looked at me with confusion.

"Can *you* see it?" She sounded frustrated, or maybe just sad.

"You give the commencement speech at NYU. You live in a small shoebox apartment, but you're happy. You actually start to write a book."

"What would I write a book about?"

"Your life."

She sipped at her coffee thoughtfully.

"I actually used to picture your life years from now. You'd marry a nice man, you'd live in the suburbs with a dog. You'll eventually have kids..."

Solene snorted.

"Sounds boring."

"What's the alternative?" Something clenched inside my throat.

"I don't know, Ara."

I was tired of wanting more from her. I left it at that. Nevermind the ache in me that begged for her to need me like I needed her.

We walked around Barcelona for hours. Solene was sober today. Our trip to New York was so close, I wasn't as frantic. Once out of Europe, would Solene feel less heavy? She'd have to get it together to maintain her scholarship. I never said this to her, but she had to have known. But then again, I felt like I couldn't even read her these days. Does she look at me and try to see inside my mind like I do to her? I hoped she saw all that I tried my best to convey. I hoped she did not see the mayhem that I hid. Horror bottle-fed me as a child and I've been burdened with a bargaining ever since. A bargaining to exhume the madwoman in me.

The last dream I ever had about the apocalypse came to me as a warning. A field topped with locusts. I'll never forget the smoke that filled the air. The feral thrum of the atmosphere. I stood there watching Solene drag a body down the hill of a beach. I didn't warn her of the trail of blood that followed behind. But I did try to cover the blood by kicking the sand over each streak. I didn't know whose body it was because it was concealed by a sheet. A sheet that was now a dark red. I didn't know a body could hold so much blood.

"Let's get her into the water. Hurry." Solene shouted over the crashing of the waves.

Was this my prison, an endless tundra of death?

"The water will just bring her back to shore."

"We have to do something. We can't just leave her."

The ground began to shake. I closed my eyes and felt my stance shift. I wanted the shaking to pass but it grew more aggressive. The gray sky then cracked open into a fiery orange color. I had to touch my face to make sure the heat wasn't melting my skin. I trudged through the sand to get to Solene, who was now clinging to the body for safety. I had always wanted to die in my sleep, peacefully. Now I was sure I would die by violence. The shaking stopped suddenly. A flock of birds flew above, their caws echoing in an unsettling way. The water, rising rapidly, was now as red as the blood that came from the body. Solene screamed and cried and I pulled her out from the water. She held onto the body but the waves took it from her in a hurry. I continued to drag her as she kicked and wailed. *I changed my mind. I want to keep her. Let me go.* She repeated this until her voice went hoarse. Once we were safe, I loosened my grasp and fell to the ground.

"What the fuck is wrong with you?" She said, "You should have left me."

"To die?"

"Yes. To die."

"Solene whose body was that?"

"We damned her." Solene said, crying once more.

"Damned who?"

"My grandmother."

"But where did all that blood come from? Vinos died

in her sleep. When we found her in that hotel room, there was no blood."

"Ara, don't you see. My grandmother will never get to heaven."

"What do you mean?"

"We didn't wash her body. We didn't wrap her in white clothes. We didn't bury her..."

"We did what we could..." I was wringing my hands, as if I was attempting to wring out the blood.

"I hate you. I hate you for making me leave her. You killed her. You did this." Solene said, quietly but foaming with hatred.

"Solene, don't leave me."

"I will not let you damn me, too."

"Solene, please."

And then in a sweltering flash, she was gone. I covered my ears as I heard what could only be the voices of at least a hundred people screeching. After the sound faded, I looked around and realized I was all alone. That's when I woke up, lurching forward in bed, breathing like I've just run a marathon. Solene was still fast asleep. I laid back down, staring at the ceiling. *I hate you for making me leave her.* I looked at my hands. They were clean. Not bloodied. I let my heart rate calm before trying to fall back asleep. The previous day I had searched *what's a proper burial for a Muslim*. Dismayed at what I found, I knew now that Solene would never forgive me or herself. All that we touched burns in hell.

I had never known a love so vast, so catastrophic and so gripping. We were a dangerous creation. A creation I was at fault for. It started in the schoolyard. It started when I saw her under the orange tree. Perhaps it started before I even knew of her existence. Did I foresee it? Did a blood pact in another life lead her to me? I can't imagine a lifetime where she doesn't get under my skin. She was the burning sensation you get when you hover your hand over a stovetop, always tempted to lay my hand down flat. Will she feel the burn too? I'd like to think we shared the same nerve endings. If I touched myself, would she know just how much I wanted her? I had never known a love that defied the gods. *But we did.* I had never known love. *Until you.*

"Is something wrong?" She asked. My hands were still wringing. Ever since my nightmare, I was on edge.

"Nothing is wrong."

"Should we do anything else before I leave for New York?"

"Before *we*."

"What?"

"You said 'before *I* leave.'" I knew I was making a big deal out of nothing. But she stared back in a way that made me question everything.

"Right. Before *we* leave." She laughed, losing that look of doubt.

"I'm sorry, I didn't sleep well." I said.

"Ara, I can't wait to go to New York with you."

I smiled.

"We can just stay in. Layla is at work. We can watch shitty movies, drink some wine, read and write." Solene suggested, kissing me on the cheek.

"Sounds perfect." I couldn't shake the feeling the dream left me with. Vinos was damned and Solene knew it. Our transgressions and all that was damaged between us was left unsaid.

I was tipsy by noon. Bringing our wine glasses into the bathroom, we filled the tub with hot water and bubbles. Climbing in together, I sunk down and felt my muscles relax. Solene wrapped her arms around me. *Her touch*, a necessary reminder for me to count my breath. To be as tender as her hands. *Her touch*, necessary.

"Every dream I have of you, it's as simple as this. You and I wrapped up in each other. I love existing with you." She whispered. I thought *every dream I have of you is overflowing with cataclysm. What does that say about me?*

I pushed aside the mountain of bubbles dividing us and kissed her. I heard water splash onto the floor. She kissed me back with a mouth tasting of wine.

"My mom warned me about making a home out of another human." Solene said.

"My mother warned me about being with a girl."

"Let's not listen to them." Solene said, tightening her arms around me. I had always wanted my mother's approval. I wanted it more than anything. But I couldn't want it and still *want* Solene. I submerged deeper into the water. My mother and Vinos, *damned*. Those words raced through my mind. I held my eyes shut as I dipped fully into the water. I counted to ten and made no attempt to come back up for air. I felt Solene tug on me. I resisted. She yanked me, hard. I came out from the water, gasping.

"Ara, what are you doing?" Solene snapped. My eyes stung from the soap. I was trying to quiet my thoughts, like that day I rolled off the dock. It wasn't a death wish, but rather a reinvention of silence.

"I was just... I don't know." There was no way around it.

"You scared me."

"Sorry. I used to do it as a kid."

"Drown yourself?"

"No." I said, defensively.

"Don't do that again." She sighed. The water was nearly cold so we got out, drying off with fluffy white towels we found in the cabinet. We read our books, naked and tangled. We were biding time. For what? I wasn't sure. I was apprehensive. I was in a paroxysm of grief. Surely she could feel it, my bones had not settled.

"*My bones are your bones, and your bones are my bones, and isn't that enough?*" Solene said. I glanced at the book she held. Ada Limon. Had she always known I considered our bones to mend as one in the chrysalis?

"*Long before I met you I had waited for you. I had always waited for you.*" Tasos Livaditis' words were all I had to say and then she was straddling me, hands enveloping every

185

inch of my body. I trembled.

"God, I can't stand it. This yearning." Solene said. She made it sound like a dirty word. *This yearning.* Was it really so bad to yearn for someone so deeply that you felt emaciated?

"Solene." Was all I could say. I could stop her and insist we talk about Rome. Insist we talk about our flaws. But she wanted to take me apart. And I let her. My mind went as silent as it was under water. I laid back on the bed and focused on the movement of our bodies. Our bodies that were designed for one another. *Our bodies*, an ancient practice. Our pleasure, centuries old. We were meant to be doing this before Eve bit the apple. After we finished, I returned to my mind. I was as torn as the meat of an orange when one was ready to eat it, to devour it, to completely engross oneself in the pulpy citrus. I missed home. I missed the weightless fog that only came with simple problems. Compared to my life since Vinos' death, I'd had it easy.

"I'm going to get more wine." Solene said. Her contempt for me, for what we did, could be felt in her mouth. With each kiss, I relived our crimes.

"Bring me some." I called out. I was ready to drink until I couldn't remember. Solene came back into the room, with two glasses full to the brim.

"I want to remember this moment forever. You, naked. Holding a wine glass while the evening sun comes in through the window." Solene said, "I want to remember everything."

I didn't like the way she was talking. As if this will be the last memory of us. I drank half the glass before speaking.

"I hope you remember everything. Down to the very first time we touched." I said, recalling when I nearly toppled over on my bike and she steadied me by *touching* my shoulder. Our first touch was of no consequence, yet I knew I would never be the same.

"I can't forget. You're a drug. Something that has entered my bloodstream. *I can't forget.*" She said, fiercely. I looked down at my wine and tried to blink away the tears that had formed. Did we both share this tormented view of love? I didn't want to be desperate. I'd rather be light and content. I didn't want to be consumed by this impulse to love *and* long *and* hunger.

When I knew my voice would be steady enough, I said "Are you using me?"

"Using you for what?"

"Sex. To numb yourself." I paused. "And *that* girl you kissed at the party..."

"You kissed her too."

"I thought that's what you wanted."

"So whatever I want, you'll just do?"

"I want to make you happy."

"One minute we're talking about *us* and then suddenly you want to pick a fight?"

"I can tell you're suffering, you're not yourself." I said, hoping she'd understand my intention.

"I feel like I'm disappearing." She admitted.

"You can talk about Rome..."

"No."

"You need to get it off your chest."

"Back off, Ara." Solene. said, standing to put on her clothes.

"I'm only trying to help."

I heard the front door open. Layla was home. I jumped up to dress myself in a hurry.

"I want to help you." I said, pulling my shirt over my head.

"Vinos is gone. What the fuck do you want me to say?" Solene shouted. I looked to the wide open door, putting a finger to my mouth to indicate that she needed to be quiet.

"Yes, she's gone." I said, "You're allowed to grieve."

"Like how you grieve your mother?" She was trying to hurt me.

"You have no idea how I've grieved my mother." I snapped.

"I know you're too scared to even keep her memory alive. Just like you're too scared to stand up to your father."

"Shut up, Solene." I murmured.

"You're so wrapped in me that you don't even realize your own fuck ups." Solene continued, her voice rising once more. "You're just as..."

"I'm just as fucked up as you are! Leaving Vinos was your idea. Not mine. And now you're taking your guilt out on me."

"You don't get to say her name." Solene looked as

angry as my father would get. I didn't recognize her.

"We left her and you never once looked back. I almost want to hate you for it." I cried out.

"Then hate me, Ara."

"I can't. That's the problem!"

I was so caught up in the moment that I didn't realize Layla was now standing in the doorway.

"Are you two okay?" She asked.

"Just say the words so I can go. Please, Ara. Hating me will make this easier." Solene said, ignoring Layla completely.

"Just go. I'm not going to say it just so your conscience is clear."

"Guys, I think we should all just take a breather." Layla said, stepping in between us.

"Leaving you will be the clearest thing I've ever done." Solene laughed harshly. The words stung but I wasn't going to let her win.

"Just fucking go, what are you waiting for?" I shouted, trying to shove past Layla to get to Solene. I wanted to push her out of the room and lock the door, pack my things and never see her again. Layla grabbed both my arms and held me back, turning to Solene.

"Maybe it's best if you go on a walk, Solene." Layla said.

"Go. I mean it." I said, seething. Solene glared at me, eyes glistening. And then she was gone. I heard the front door slam with a bang.

"Are you okay?" Layla said, letting me go. I had just realized I was visibly shaking.

"I'm fine." I said, sitting on the edge of the bed to find some stability. I was on the verge of puking, my vision now blurry. I didn't want to give Solene the satisfaction of crying. "I'm fine." I repeated.

"Do you want me to leave you alone?"

I nodded.

She walked out, closing the door behind her. The silence of the room was now an open wound. I laid down, curling into a ball. I could feel a throbbing plea to find the strength to get up and leave. Leave for good. I couldn't. I was preserved in my own longing. Solene had taken so much from me. I can't seem to remember what she had taken. My innocence? It was already long gone before I knew her. My sanity? I'm not sure if it was ever there to begin with.

It was two a.m. when I heard the bedroom door open. I was still holding my knees to my chest. I knew it was Solene because her presence was a death march. She was here to say goodbye. I closed my eyes, pretending to be asleep. As if sleep could prolong the ending.

"Ara." Solene said. I felt a dip in the mattress as she crawled onto the bed. "Wake up."

"No." I said, keeping my eyes shut tight.

"You're so stubborn."

"If you came back just to insult me some more..." I began. I felt her hand grip my arm.

"I am fucked up." Solene said.

I stayed silent as she rested her chin on my shoulder.

"Ever since Rome, I've been filled with so much rage…"

"That you don't know where to put it?"

"Yes." She whispered. Her breathing turned ragged. She was crying. I finally opened my eyes, turning to face her. I put my forehead to hers.

"I'm filled with so much rage, I can taste it like blood in my mouth." I said.

"Let me carry it for you." She sobbed. I shook my head.

"You'll end up resenting me."

She swallowed. "I feel as if I already resent you."

I knew it was coming. A confessional. A confession of *I love you but it's all too much.*

"Do you resent me for what happened in Rome?"

"We left her there. We just left her." She was now sobbing uncontrollably. I held her, letting her tears burn into my skin. I couldn't fix this. The knife was already too deep in both our backs. "I've lost myself in you."

"I'm sorry." An apology was all I could offer.

"Kiss me." She insisted. I made no argument. I kissed her with remorse. She kissed me back in a dangerous frenzy. It scared me. I was becoming nothing more than ashes.

"Solene, I love…"

"Don't you dare." Solene said. "Don't say you love me."

"I do, I do." I continued to burn. "You won't find another person who loves you more."

"I'm leaving *you*." She said, kissing me one last time on the mouth. I didn't know whose tears belonged to who. I felt the mixture grow into an ocean.

191

"Solene, please."

"I'm sorry. I'm sorry. I'm sorry." She said until it didn't sound like a word anymore. "I have a ticket for you to fly back to America. You have to take the train to the airport. I'll leave you with as much money as you need."

"Is this some sort of sick joke?" She must have had this planned for days.

"I can't do this. Not with you. I love you, but it's killing me." Solene said. "What I did for *us* is unforgivable."

"Solene, I'm begging you."

I felt her touch disappear as she walked away. She was gone before I could get another word in. I didn't run after her. I didn't shout her name. She didn't even look back. I was left in the dark room. I could only hear a dreadful thumping in my chest. I wanted to throw a tantrum as a child would. I was not a child. I was not anything. And in the quiet of that dark room, my disembodied self grew to love the moon as I watched it from the window. I didn't move from that spot until morning.

Layla was gone when I finally arose. The tickets for the flight and train were laying on top of my bag. I was tempted to rip them up. Instead, I packed my bags calmly and left the apartment. The day was bright and hot. I looked around at all the people walking, living, and breathing. *Did they not know the world was ending?* Everything sounded like white noise. The walk to the train station was grueling and I could feel what could only be barbed wire clench around my heart.

I ignored it. I was determined to bleed out.

I rode on the train, fragmentary images whirling past. I couldn't cry, I couldn't even open my mouth to let out a noise resembling pain. I was deprived of emotion, anesthetized. Reaching for my phone in my pocket, I went rigid. Solene took my phone weeks ago. I was left with nothing. No way to reach her. And now, in an unfamiliar country, all alone, I thought to myself *None of this should have happened.* Leaving Vinos behind was in vain. There was no point to Rome. No point to Spain. No point to New York. No point in loving *her*.

To love someone deranges you. I could hardly stand it. I walked off the train and found my way to the entrance of the airport. I was suddenly ill, dropping my bags to the ground, I attempted to breathe but I was left without air. A stranger ran to my side. Others around me looked with worry but kept on walking. After I settled down, I showed the stranger my flight information and they led me to my terminal. I was moved by their humanity. Saying goodbye, I turned to board my flight, ready for anything but this suffocation.

I slept the entire flight, grateful for the freedom from my mind. A mind that now coexisted with Solene and a newfound grief. I had always held grief in my hands, but Solene had never been the one I was grieving. I had nearly a lifetime's worth of familiarity to grieve now. We were familiar, from the very beginning. Knowing which sweet spots to touch, knowing when to listen and nurture.

Knowing each other down to the very core. In the end, we will become nothing more than strangers. I will catch the scent of cinnamon and I will be reminded of her. I will watch the early morning sun pulsating light and I will be reminded of her. Every detail woven into this life will *remind me* until I can no longer remember for the both of us.

I landed in California with womanhood dead at my feet. I will turn eighteen tomorrow but I feel no different. I was right back where I started. I only knew my father's number, so I punched it bitterly into the nearest phone I found.

"Hello?"

I almost felt relief. He sounded sober, like the father who once raised me.

"Dad..."

"Ara?"

"Please don't be mad." I whispered.

"Are you okay? Where are you?"

"I'm at the airport. Can you come get me?"

"Tell me you're okay."

I closed my eyes.

"Dad, I'm so sorry." And it was in that airport where I began to cry on the phone with my father. I didn't care who saw me.

"It's okay. I'm on my way, sweetheart."

I hung up the phone and walked to the pickup zone. I stood there, isolated from the world. I stood there and let the sun dry my eyes. I stood there, head tilted to the sky and thought, *I can't do this*. I believed that love was *not* for the fragile. That was until she loved me softly. I *now* believed love was a murderous thing, a testament to breaking bones and wheat fields that burned whenever I was touched. None of it's real. There's no magic, fate or god. There's no more oranges to eat, no more poetry to write, and no more *how soon can you get to my house*. I was a burial ground for our memories. Despite this, I will still try my best to be kind, I will eat three meals, I will carry on each day with an ardent heart. I *can* love the little things. And I will *learn* to not live so animalistically. I will, I will.

part three

"I am living. I remember you."

— Marie Howe, What the living do

Chapter thirteen

and the ashes rest in a common urn

10 years later

The alarm went off at its usual time, seven a.m. And I groan in the usual way, rolling over to turn it off. I was severely hungover, already dreading the flashbacks of the night before. It wasn't like me to drink a lot, not since my father hit his ninety days of sobriety years ago. I wanted to be supportive. But my week warranted a night of drinking. Maybe even a random hookup. Who knows. I looked around the room. I was naked and alone. I couldn't remember if anyone came home with me. It's been two months since I broke up with my last girlfriend so a little sex couldn't hurt. Her voice was now in my head *you can't stand being alone, you'll die wrapped around someone's thumb*. I got up out of bed with resentment, stretched, and then made my way to the kitchen for some coffee. I let out a little scream when I saw a girl walk out from the bathroom, wearing my baggy t-shirt I've had since I was a teenager. The yelp must've made me look pathetic.

"Sorry, I didn't know anyone was here." I said, painfully aware of just how naked I was.

"That's okay." She smiled. "I was a little confused when I woke up too."

"Did we...?"

"Sleep together? Yeah."

I looked her up and down.

"Nice." I said. She looked good in my t-shirt. "I'm going to get dressed. Want some coffee?"

"Sure."

I threw on whatever I could find on the floor of my bedroom and walked back out into the kitchen where she was now sitting.

"Ara, right?"

"Yeah. Yours? I can't recall a thing. Don't hate me." I laughed nervously. She laughed back as if to reassure me there were no hard feelings.

"Molly."

Molly was ginger, with an array of freckles covering her fair skin. I couldn't help but stare at her pink lips. She was definitely my type. With her long legs, green eyes, and confident way she was leaning against my counter; it was no surprise she spent the night at my place.

"I just got out of a two year relationship..."

"I know." Molly said, "You wouldn't stop talking about her. Hurts a girl's ego."

"Sorry..."

"Solene really did a number on you."

I dropped the mug I was holding, hearing the loud clash of the dish breaking onto the marble. I hardly felt the burn of the scalding coffee that was now at my feet.

"Her name was Evelyn."

"Whose?"

"My ex of two years." I said, grabbing a towel to push the shards of ceramic into the trash. Molly pursed her lips.

"Well whoever Solene was, you wouldn't shut up about her."

I looked at her blankly.

"Which I didn't mind. You just seemed…"

"I have a meeting in an hour. I should shower."

"I'll show myself out." Molly said. Minutes passed and she came back out of my room, wearing a black jumpsuit. She really was stunning.

"Want to exchange numbers?" I said, noncommittal.

"I had a lot of fun." Molly smiled. "But I think we should just leave it at that."

I agreed. I didn't want to bring her into my mess. A life that I could barely keep together. We hugged and then she was out the door. I really did have a meeting and now I was running late.

The city was a living thing. I felt its heartbeat while walking down Pike, its pulse on Madison. I was most like myself in this city. My lungs, less strained despite the upward climb it took to get here. *Here* as in, I am happy but still learning what that means. Evelyn told me I'd never know happiness, even if it bit me in the ass. She had every right to say it. I was a horrible girlfriend.

"She was so in love with you. That's all I'm saying." Samantha said. I was on 2nd Street, waiting for the crosswalk sign. I adjusted my earbuds and sighed.

199

"I wasn't feeling it." I simply stated.

"After two whole years?"

"Yeah. I mean, I just hooked up with this girl last night and I didn't even miss her. Does that make me a soulless bitch?"

"Who the hell did you hook up with?"

"Some girl named Molly. I met her at a party."

"God, maybe I should come to Seattle. I haven't been laid in months."

"Please do. I'm lonely." I laughed, turning the corner and stopping outside a tall brown building.

"You've been living there for years now and you still haven't made a single friend. You need to make an effort." Samantha said like a stern mother.

"I have this meeting I have to get to. Talk to you later?" I said. She said her goodbye as I hung up. Putting my phone into my pocket, I jogged up the steps and opened the tall wooden door. I made it with time to spare. I was dreading going into the next room, knowing they'd be demanding a new poetry book. I hadn't written anything in months. I forgot what it's like to have a muse, my sense of love was nonexistent. I hadn't truly found another to be myself around, to laugh with and put down my guard. But with my job and this city, I could at least leave my apartment and have a purpose. I could at least say I was living.

After my meetings, I had a certain ritual. I always went to the gym, stopped to buy a protein shake, went grocery shopping, and ended the night with a homemade meal and wrote until I fell asleep. Since the writing wasn't panning out, I'd usually just stare at my laptop until I began to nod off. Sometimes I'd take a bath with a good book. Sometimes I'd watch shitty T.V. Sometimes I even masturbated out of pure boredom. Tonight wasn't any different. I turned off the current reality show I was watching and got up to find a snack. I ate a handful of almonds and wrote a single line down in my journal. *Note to self: I have not forgotten what love feels like, I have just chosen to diminish what it means to be loved.* My phone began to buzz. I glanced down and saw it was my father.

"Hey dad."

"Hi kiddo. Hope it's not too late for me to call."

"No, you're fine."

"I just wanted to see how you're holding up, after everything with... Evelyn." He said her name like it was taboo. I looked at my fridge and noticed a picture of Evelyn and I still hanging there. I removed the magnet, took the picture into my hand and crumpled it up.

"I'm actually great. The breakup was just what I needed."

"You're a strong one, Ara. I'm proud of you." He cleared his throat. It's been months since I've been out to visit him in California. He moved to another town awhile back and he met someone named Debbie. I was thrilled he turned his life around. Though there were ups and downs with his sobriety, I still cherished our newfound relationship.

"Thanks, Dad. How are you and Debbie?"

"We're great. I just hit 5 years of sobriety today."

"Dad, I'm so happy for you." I was honestly choked up. I never thought I'd get him back.

"I couldn't have done it without you." He said, a smile apparent in his voice. I smiled too. After the phone call, I went back to my journal and continued to write until three a.m. It was nothing of significance, but it was the start of something I could be proud of. Despite what Samantha said, I *was* lonely, but in love with a life I never thought I'd have. In love with *something*, rather than a person. I was finally free.

Therapy was in an hour. I was someone who goes to therapy. I resisted it for years but now I couldn't imagine any other version of myself without it. My therapist's name was Shaina. A middle aged woman who has gone through two divorces, lost custody of her child, and drives a Toyota. It helped to have a therapist who understood pain just as much as any other person. Who wants a therapist who has a picturesque life? She's the one who suggested that I break up with Evelyn after I confessed that I felt like the relationship was stripping me down to nothing. "I've always felt nothing. My whole life. But since moving to Seattle, I noticed that *nothing* was incredibly dull." Shaina understood me. She understood what I needed in order to be content. Abrasive at times, I didn't mind when she called me out on my bullshit. "I have everything I want." I said during a session where I was soaked from the rain that I walked in to get here. "Everything?" She said, squinting her eyes at me. "Yep." I said. "I don't believe you. Your homework is to go home and think about it." She said, writing down what I guessed to be a literal scribble into her pad of paper. "There's nothing to think about." I shrugged. "Would the name Solene bring anything up for you?" She said, adjusting her glasses that slipped to the bridge of her nose. "I'm not here to talk about her." I said, gripping the arms of my chair, my nails embedded into them. I didn't think about anything after that session and I didn't schedule another appointment for nearly three weeks. But today, of all days, I was eager to march into that room and prove to her I was right. *I have everything I want.*

"Ara, come in." Shaina said from her doorway, smiling. I sat down in the chair across from her and watched her as she watched me. "I didn't think I'd see you again."

"Sorry, I've been busy. Book deadlines and all."

"Glad to hear you're writing again."

"I broke up with Evelyn."

"Oh?"

"She took it well. I mean, if you don't count the fact that she told me I didn't know how to function without loving another person."

"How did that make you feel?"

I snorted at the cliché.

"I think she's a liar." I said.

"You didn't even think that maybe she, as your lover, might know you well?"

203

"She only knew parts of me.

"Why's that?" She scribbled onto her pad.

"Look, I didn't do your homework from last session. But Molly said..."

"Who's Molly?"

I blushed.

"Just a girl I met. She said when I was drunk I wouldn't stop talking about *Solene*."

"And?"

"And I don't like that I talked about *her*. I want to know why that happened. So tell me why and how to fix it."

"You'd know if you did your homework." Shaina smiled.

"Fine. I'll do the homework." I groaned.

"When you get home, think about Solene and why it didn't work out. Go over every detail you can remember and ask yourself *is she someone I want in my life?*"

"But I don't want her in my life."

"Exactly! Use memory to remind your psyche that she's someone who doesn't belong in your life."

"So..."

"Open old wounds to learn from them." She said, closing her notepad. I nodded, not convinced. Solene wasn't a memory I wanted dug back up. But there were times, times I told no one about, where I'd see someone with hazel hair and feel like I can't go on. I'd hear Arabic and I couldn't figure out what this awful ache was. Even at the grocery store, in the produce section, I'd find myself holding a giant

plump orange and I'd think *fucking fuck*. And then I'd leave
the grocery store empty handed. *Fuck.*

I ate my handful of almonds that night, sitting down
on my unmade bed. Pretending to be the healed version of
myself was hard. I ate these almonds because I didn't want
to gain weight. I didn't write as much anymore because all
I wanted to write about was *her*. And I sure as hell didn't
pray because I only heard my mother's voice in my head. It
freaked me out. Not even Shaina knew these things about
me. I was twenty eight and I had no idea what I was made up
of besides atoms. I wanted to bend the rules and tell Shaina I
got home and wrote all night about how Solene was my one
great love and I'm never getting that back and that was okay.
I clenched my jaw. I just wanted to sleep. Sitting back into
my pile of pillows, I closed my eyes. *Remember the long walk
we took from the cafe to the lake? Remember the time we stole
your grandmother's wine? Remember when you said you could
never leave me even held at gunpoint and I laughed and you
stayed dead serious. Remember the names we picked out for our
kids? I never asked you if you thought I'd make a good mother.
Remember how I would kiss your neck just to hear that certain
sound you made? Remember, remember, remember when I bit
your lip on accident and I didn't mind the blood in my mouth?
I hope it all will come back to you in violent waves.* I opened
my eyes back up. It was dark outside and raining as usual. I
brushed my teeth and undressed slowly. I didn't mind that
my queen sized bed was only occupied by me. I didn't mind

anything. I was fine. *And when I think I'm fine, I'll want you suddenly and inescapably.*

I went to tend to my wounds like a stray mutt. Shaina said I would find the answer in them, but instead I see God in every wound. It does not heal. A wound does not forget his wrath. Neither does it forget my own fury. Even after all these years I was still a woman-made dam, built to hold in rage. It bursts, a thumb to a pomegranate. It bursts and my hysteria eats itself as an earthworm does the soil. I am plagiarized by the very grief I've so desperately fought to become.

"Okay I admit it, I'm not over her."

"Not over Solene?"

"Yes. I see her everywhere."

"Interesting." Shaina said, taking her pen out from behind her ear to scribble down some more nonsense. I imagined it would say *Not over an ex she hasn't seen in 10 years. Pathetic.*

"Interesting?"

"Have you thought about reaching out to her...for closure?" Shaina said, crossing her legs and setting aside her notepad.

"Fuck no." I cleared my throat. "I mean, no. I would never."

"What do you think you need to move on then? It's certainly not *time*. Did you do your homework?"

"Yeah."

"And?"

Sometimes she pushed me to my limit and I felt like screaming.

"I learned nothing. I just opened a wound and now I'm a fountain pouring out years of suppressed longing." I didn't mean to sound like a soapbox. I covered my face with my hands and sighed.

"Ara, you learned something." Shaina said, softly. "You learned that you still want someone who hurt you tremendously. When we first met, you talked about Solene as if she was just a thing of the past. I could barely get anything out of you. But now you can *focus* on a future that doesn't involve her."

"How? How can I possibly move on after years of loving her? I don't even know who she is anymore but she's sabotaged every romantic relationship I've ever had. What if it turns out I'm just this insane, obsessive girl who..."

"You need closure, Ara." Shaina said, resolutely. "Whether it be closure from her or finding that in yourself, I promise you you can live a long, full life. Free from Solene."

I was in Rome again. I was in California. I was in that alleyway where we left Vinos. I ran a shaky hand through my hair and looked at Shaina.

"What if I don't want to move on?" I said. I was a successful author. I lived in my dream city, along with my dream apartment. The air outside smelled of the sea and baked almonds. I had all that I needed, down to the very relationship I had with my father. But the question still tugged at me, maliciously. Will I be alone for the rest of my life?

"I know you want to move on because you wouldn't be so miserable if that wasn't the case." Shaina said. She was so wise at times, I wanted to roll my eyes.

"Closure?" I said.

She nodded.

I don't even know what that meant for someone like me. I can't even sleep next to another body without wishing it to be Solene. Evelyn wasn't the first one I broke up with. There was Rachel, Tara and Tegan. All deemed serious relationships that I screwed up. *You don't know how to love someone,* Tara said. Rachel was the one who said *I don't know what demons you have, but you better fix them before choosing to love another human.* Tegan was the one who just cried and begged for me to stay. I'll never forget when she said *You and I, we're people who can't be alone. You'll just go to the next girl and the next and the next, and you'll burn everything in your wake.*

It was midnight when I chose to Facetime Samantha. She answered with a groggy look. I should have felt bad for waking her, but I was desperate to talk to someone.

"Is everything okay?" Samantha said, voice still masked with sleep.

"Sam." I paused, "I know you follow her on Instagram."

"Follow who?"

"Solene." I hadn't said a single word about Solene since

returning from Spain. She was our unspoken rule of *don't ask*.

"Ara, what the fuck. It's twelve at night. Why are you even thinking about her?"

"I'm sorry for waking you." I said, "But I need to know. How is she?"

Samantha looked at me, cautiously.

"She's good. She's, um, getting married." Samantha said.

"Oh."

"Fuck, I shouldn't have said anything..."

"Who is she marrying?"

"Some guy, I don't know. Ara, I'm not going to torture you with the details. You have a good life in Seattle. When you came back from Europe, you were at your lowest. I never asked but I know Solene did something to break your heart. You deserve better."

"I have to go." I whispered.

"Ara..."

"I'm sorry for calling so late. Talk to you tomorrow?" I hung up before she could protest. I wanted to throw my phone at the wall. Engaged. *To some guy.* I got up to go into the kitchen, snatching my only bottle of red wine. I put the bottle to my mouth and met her mouth in the same instance. I drank until I grew sick.

I woke up with a pounding headache. I sauntered to the bathroom, grimacing at my red stained lips and the mess of my hair. I had no meetings today. I could sleep all day. I could go to the liquor store. I could call Shaina and tell her I was having a crisis. *You started this. You told me to open old wounds.* I picked up my phone and saw three missed calls and four text messages, all from Samantha.

Ara, are you okay?

I shouldn't have told you.

Call me.

Do I need to come to Seattle?

I texted her back with *Come to Seattle.*

It was raining outside and I needed to do my usual routine. Gym, grocery shop, write. But I felt like Solene was out there, somewhere close. I could feel it. After Sam and I went over the details of her coming to visit, I brushed my teeth until the taste of wine was completely gone and I brushed my hair until it was smooth. My desire was still in Metamorphosis. A knife in my side, it twists. I left my apartment and walked out onto the street, glancing around before I made my way to the market. I planted a garden to become myself again. I did, I became myself and even more than that. I also planted a garden for this yearning and it turned into a grave. A shallow one. It was now back from the dead. I stood outside the market for minutes before turning around and heading in the wrong direction. I walked for miles. All the way up Pine until I reached Capitol Hill. I stopped by a nearby cafe, got a black coffee and took out my journal I always carried with me in my bag. I wrote *I'm daydreaming about you. Again. I'm daydreaming and I'm tired. I'd like to be the language we invented. I'd like to be heavenly as you made me out to be. I said there was no such thing. I should've known better than to question a god that created you.* I closed the journal. I walked to the nearest bookstore, browsing the poetry section. My book was on the middle shelf. I picked it up and flicked to a random page. I rolled my eyes and set it back on the shelf. I imagined Solene reading my book with disgust. I chose to immortalize *us*. Will she feel it on every page? Will she feel the tenderness I chose to communicate through every word? The tenderness now lethal, it was a book of mourning. I had this sudden urge to stalk all her socials but I was blocked. I've been blocked since Spain. I took out my phone and thought about calling Evelyn to tell her it wasn't true. I did know how to be alone. I thought about walking around the city until I found Solene. But she was far away. In an unknown place. Probably New York. By the time I left the bookstore it was pouring. So I walked home in the rain, wishing it would cleanse me of this resurgence. *The resurgence of Solene, Solene, Solene.* The holy name I kept in the back of my mouth, only to say it in the quiet of a room. But of course, as with any thought of Solene came the thought of Vinos, and the fact that I now question if my safety was truly the reason for leaving her body. Ever since Spain, I couldn't help but put the pieces together and realize that her motives may have been disconnected from what she had insisted. Yet I can't blame her. I too was at fault for not seeing the warning signs. I can't help but admit that I would do it all again because I really did believe that our

211

love was tangible.

I picked Samantha up at the airport later that week, hugging her tight as she got into the passenger seat. It had been months since we last saw each other.

"Work was okay with you coming here?"

"I can work from my laptop." She shrugged.

"How are you?" I asked.

"I'm good. How are you?"

"I'm good."

Our small talk was fake. I knew she wanted answers. She wanted to know why the sudden interest in Solene's life. I could lie and say it was curiosity. But we both know it's because I never let things go. I still actively imagine the room where I found my mother. I still flinch when someone raises their voice. I still eat a handful of almonds for dessert. Once at my apartment, I offered her a glass of wine and she eyed it like it was poisoned.

"I thought you didn't drink anymore?"

"I drink every now and then."

"We should talk about... Solene." Samantha said, her mouth at the brim of the glass. She said *her* name as if to test my reaction. I remained stoic.

"Can I see her fiance?" I asked.

"Ara, I want to know why you're asking about her? After all these years..."

"You'll laugh."

"Try me."

I finished off my wine and set down the glass with steadiness. I was learning to be steadier. I had to learn. My lack of steadiness bred a girl who took apart their own happiness with shaky hands.

"I can't imagine a life where I'm not in love with her." I said, slowly.

"You're living a life, right now, where you *should* be out of love with her. It's been years. You've been doing okay without her." Samantha said, sliding over her glass of wine to me.

"Why do I feel this way then? Why do I hope to see her in every girl I meet?"

"Is this why you dumped Evelyn?"

"I dumped Evelyn because I lost feelings for her..."

"Because you still have feelings for Solene?" Samantha said, her face contorted into a look of confusion.

"You have no idea what happened between Solene and I in Rome. No idea."

"Tell me."

"I can't."

"Look, I still think about my first love... sometimes. It's normal."

"I don't just *sometimes* think about her, Sam." I sighed. "Show me a picture."

Samantha hesitantly pulled out her phone. After a moment of typing, she handed it to me. My eyes immediately fell onto Solene. Her hair was longer, just as hazel. I could feel the warmth of her skin through the screen. Her smile was genuine, lips full and teeth white. Her hands were wrapped around a tall man. He had light brown hair, slightly curly. His jaw was angular. Blue eyes. Both their freckles were shown by the sun they stood under. They stood in a green field, surrounded by lilies. It was an engagement announcement. Henry. That was his name. I handed back the phone to her and finished off the second glass of wine.

"They look happy." I murmured. Samantha looked at me with pity as I poured another glass. "I need closure. That's what my therapist says."

"Do you want her number?"

"No. I can't contact her." I said, imagining my tight grip shattering the wine glass. "Do you want to sleep in my bed or the couch? I'll get you some blankets."

I couldn't sleep. Samantha passed out as soon as her head hit the pillow. I was alone with my thoughts. I couldn't stand it. I tiptoed out of my bedroom and sat down on the couch. I knew exactly who I wanted to talk to.

Can I call?

I bit my nails as I stared at my phone, waiting for a reply. Ten minutes passed and my phone finally buzzed.

"Hello."

"Ara, is everything okay?" My father sounded concerned.

"I can't sleep."

"Anything on your mind?"

"Do you remember when I came back to America, after I ran away?"

"Vividly." He paused, "I couldn't get you out of bed for months."

"I never told you what happened... Solene left me. In Spain. She broke up with me and left."

"Have you talked to her since?"

"No." I think I might die if I ever saw her again. "Dad, I don't know how to move on. I lost the love of my life. What if I never find that again?"

"I know I wasn't a great example in the face of moving on..." My father said, his voice catching.

"You did what you could. You also lost the love of your life..."

"And then I met Debbie."

"Does it even compare?" I was crying now.

"Yes, Ara. Yes and you can find it, too."

"How? How do I move on without closure?" I said, attempting to gasp for air.

"Listen to me. I had to learn this the hard way. You don't need closure to move on. Closure happens when it ends amicably. Not all of us are lucky enough for that ending, but all we can do is just *move on*. The goodbye wasn't ideal? Move on *anyways*. I promise you if closure was all we needed, then heartbreak would almost be non-existent. You feel this way because she changed you. She carved a meaning into your life that you have yet to find. Don't waste this lesson on pining. Use it to create, show new lovers what it's like. Don't waste her absence on grief. She did not die. Don't waste this love on sadness. She did not wish you ill. She left. She simply

215

chose to move on first. Now it's your turn. Closure is not a guarantee. But do you know what is? The courage to heal all on your own. That courage takes time. Solene made you brave the moment she decided to leave. Don't spend time trying to make sense of loss. Life is full of it. We can only keep it for so long. Don't waste this lesson, Ara. Don't waste it like I did after your mother died."

My body made a safe space for grief to occupy. I nurtured that space for I was at a loss on how to heal. Healing wasn't a quick fix for someone like me. I steeped in grief, I pondered it, and I wandered through it with a light. I carried a torch for a frazzled love that begged to be put down. I carried a torch for all the girls who have picked at my bones. I carried myself across each border of holy ground. And I carried on with a decaying sense of self. I thought, *nobody is safe from the grief that comes with losing yourself in another person.* But now, as I stood on the corner of Union Street, I watched the red hand flash. When it changed to a walk signal, I did not move. I stepped back and removed my hood as the rain began to soak my hair and face. I did not move. I watched others pass me. A car in the distance pulled up to the curb and a woman stepped out. I saw her side profile, her long dark hair, her tall slender body. Perhaps it was Solene. I walked in the direction of the vehicle. Perhaps I was imagining things. I edged closer to the woman, her laughter like bells as a man took her hand. With a single glance over her shoulder, our eyes met. Solene. Solene.

Solene. *Was it you?* The woman continued on as I stood in place. Her figure began to fade within the rain and distance. My legs, with a mind of their own, chose to follow her. I walked and walked, my heart racing. I should turn around. I should call out her name. With indecision, I halted and watched her. *Was it you?* The sound of the city gave no answers. A cyclist rode past me in a blur. A man stopped a passerby and asked for money. The smell of cinnamon from a nearby food stand swam through the air. I saw the woman look back at me. And then I was alive, breathing without her. I was erased from her existence.

But if you need reminding of the orange tree, I will remind you. And if you need help in the next life to find me, I will want to run the other way. *I won't.* I remember the apocalypse as if it were yesterday; melting sidewalks, the swallowing sea, a field to burn in with you. I can go on and on with my rehearsal of meeting you once more, but I can't carry you much longer. Within the turbulence of your heart, I hope you knew just how heavy your name was when I held it in my lungs.

Acknowledgements

Thank you to my partner for all their love and endless support, for being the one who witnessed my process from the very beginning. Thank you to Bryce Murphy, my editor, best friend, and the one who I told this story to years ago. His encouragement and willingness to bring this to life inspired me and I couldn't be more grateful. Thank you to Ammar Al-Saffar for his constant feedback, editing, and friendship. I wouldn't be the author that I am without him. Thank you to my friends and family. Thank you to Birdie Maxwell for their brilliant artistry. Their art can be found on the title page and Instagram: miss.understood_galleries. Finally, my deepest thanks to my Grandpa, Glen Nelson, for painting the beautiful cover to this book. His art and talent never ceases to amaze me. I love you, Grandpa.

Milton Keynes UK
Ingram Content Group UK Ltd.
UKHW040133021124
2510UKWH00042B/45

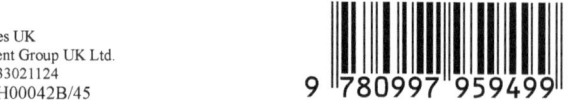